# When the Streets Clap Back

Lock Down Publications and Ca$h
Presents

# When the Streets Clap Back

A Novel by *Jibril Williams*

# Lock Down Publications

P.O. Box 870494
Mesquite, Tx 75187

**Lock Down Publications**
**Like our page on Facebook: Lock Down Publications @**
www.facebook.com/lockdownpublications.ldp
Cover design and layout by: **Dynasty Cover Me**
Book interior design by: **Shawn Walker**
Edited by: **Tisha Andrews**

# Stay Connected with Us!

Text **LOCKDOWN** to 22828 to stay up-to-date with new releases, sneak peaks, contests and more...

Thank you!

## Submission Guideline.

Submit the first three chapters of your completed manuscript to ldpsubmissions@gmail.com, subject line: Your book's title. The manuscript must be in a .doc file and sent as an attachment. Document should be in Times New Roman, double spaced and in size 12 font. Also, provide your synopsis and full contact information. If sending multiple submissions, they must each be in a separate email.

Have a story but no way to send it electronically? You can still submit to LDP/Ca$h Presents. Send in the first three chapters, written or typed, of your completed manuscript to:

LDP: Submissions Dept
Po Box 870494
Mesquite, Tx 75187

*DO NOT send original manuscript. Must be a duplicate.*

Provide your synopsis and a cover letter containing your full contact information.

Thanks for considering LDP and Ca$h Presents.

# Chapter 1

"Everyone in this bitch, put your fucking hands on your head and don't move. I said don't fucking move. Now, we all know what the fuck this is. If I see you reach, move or even sneeze, I'ma put a hole in your head!" Skalez yelled to the four hustlers in the house that he and his boys had just ran in.

Block and 40 went and checked the four hustlers to see if they had any guns on them. Only two of them were strapped. While Block and 40 patted them down, Skalez had the chopper AK-47 pointed at them just in case one of them tried to be Superman. In that case, they would only end up super fucked.

"Is there anyone else in here?" Skalez asked, making sure there weren't any unexpected guests. Every one of them said 'no' in unison.

"All right, every last one of you niggas lay face down slowly. I said slowly, nigga," Skalez yelled to the big nigga that was moving too fast.

"I got bad nerves, so don't temp me. My finger is already itching. Block, go check the rest of the house to see if there's anyone else in this bitch. You already know what to say when you find what we came for. 40, go in these niggas' pockets," Skalez said, telling the men what to do. He was calling the shots.

As he looked down on the four guys that lay across the floor, he saw the way they all were looking scared to death.

"You niggas know what we came for. We see y'all bagging up on the able and shit. Where the rest of the shit at?" Skalez asked, raising his voice.

"That's all we got left. We was about to re-up after we got off of this," the big nigga said, speaking for the group.

"Oh yeah? Well damn! I guess we came at the wrong time, huh? We should just leave and come back after y'all re-up, huh?" Skalez said, with growing sarcasm. "How much work is that on the table?" Skalez asked.

"One brick," the big nigga answered.

"40, go wrap that up and throw it in the bag. A'ight, where the money at?" As soon as Skalez asked the question, he heard what he'd been waiting to hear.

"Jackpot," Block yelled twice, informing Skalez and 40 he had hit the stash. He then came back in the front room and told them where he found the safe.

"All right, which one of you niggas know the combination?" Skalez asked, waving the AK-47 at all them. No one responded. "Ok, so y'all wanna play the quiet game, huh?"

As soon as he said that, 40 started hitting one of the vics with his 40 cal, splitting the side of his face.

The guy started yelling, "I don't know it." The other guys were looking, scared to death at their partner as blood started leaking from his face.

"I know the combination," the big man said, hoping it all would all be over soon. Little did he know, he had just signed his own death certificate.

Skalez started smiling, pointing the AK-47 at his head. "I knew you knew something when you was doing all the talking in this bitch. Now, lead me to the money trail, big man, before I paint these walls in here red with your head.

"40, come with me. Block, make sure these niggas don't turn into track stars and try to do the hundred-yard dash on us."

Block also had a chopper and Skalez knew he wouldn't hesitate to let it off. As they made it to the room in the back of the house, the big man went to the closet and knelt down to turn the knob on the safe.

"40, go on his right side and put the 40 cal to his head," Skalez said. "Don't try nothing, you fuck."

Skalez stood behind the big nigga with the barrel of that AK-47 to the back of his head. The big nigga began to shake.

He had fucked up, trying to open the safe twice, but the third time he opened it.

Skalez told him to back away and lay face down. As he did that, 40 kept his three eyes on him, two on his face and one in his hand. Skalez took the bag from across his shoulders and started throwing the stacks in. As he placed the last couple of stacks in the bag, he heard a sound.

*Tat! Tat!Tat!*

*I know the sound of that,* Skalez thought.

"Hurry up! We gotta roll out!" Blocked yelled.

"Please don't do this," the big man started, pleading on the floor. "Don't kill me, man."

Before he could utter another word, Skalez let off two slugs in his head. Skalez then picked up the bag full of money, then he and 40 ran to the front room where they saw three dead bodies. Block was taking off a chain from one of the guy's neck.

"This Jesus piece couldn't save your ass from this," Block said out loud to the dead body he had taken the chain from. Then he stood up and fired one more shot into each of them before leaving.

"Man, bring your ass on," Skalez yelled to Block. Then they ran out the front door and hopped in the stolen Town and Country van. The houses weren't close by far, but Skalez knew someone had to hear the shots. When they drove down the street and turned the corner to the main road, they all took their ski masks off.

"A yo, how much you think we got off them niggas?" Block asked.

"I don't know. We gon' do the math when we get to the hotel room," Skalez replied.

"Yo Skalez, I saw you smiling hard up under that mask when that big nigga opened that safe, too," 40 said, laughing.

"I'm surprised them bullets killed that big ass nigga. I thought I was gonna have to let the whole clip go," Skalez replied, not really paying attention to what 40 just said.

"Yeah, that was a big mu'fucker," Block added.

"Man, that nigga looked like Biggie Smalls on steroids," 40 said, joking. Block and Skalez started laughing.

When they got to the hotel room, Skalez dumped all the money, coke and guns on the bed. Block and 40 reached for the two guns while Skalez reached for what people kill for every day, that paper.

"All right, look here, you gun happy ass niggas. Let's count this money so we can be up out of this bitch." Skalez began separating the bills in denominations.

An hour later, they had counted the money, which totaled forty-five thousand dollars evenly.

"Damn, we been laying on these niggas for two and a half weeks and that's all they had? Shit, we should've took them niggas trucks that was out front and took 'em to Lil John's chop shop," 40 told them, a little angry about the money.

"We bodied them niggas for this?" Block said, looking at the money.

"Shit, bodies come cheaper than that nowadays," Skalez said seriously.

"No doubt," Block agreed.

"Shit, I ain't gon' do nothing but put some rims on the Lex and a new system in the joint!" Block said after they split the money up three ways evenly, totaling fifteen thousand a piece.

"What we gon' do about the work?" 40 asked Skalez, not really paying Block any mind.

"Just hold it until tomorrow. As a matter of fact, dude said that was a whole joint, so just bring 12 ounces tomorrow. You and Block do what y'all want with y'all half," Stalez told them.

"That's what's up," 40 replied, then looked at Block adjusting the chain around his neck.

"Damn, Block. That nigga ain't been dead three hours and you rocking that nigga's chain like it's yours."

"First off, I don't give a fuck if that nigga only been dead less than a New York minute and two seconds. And I'm not wearing it like it's mine, dumbass nigga, because it is mine! Shit, it looks better on me anyway. I'll never let a nigga look better than me in my own shit," Block replied, being humorous, but serious at the same time.

"You two niggas a trip. I'm outta here. Dump that van when you two check out of this place," Skalez said before he left.

# Chapter 2

As Skalez cruised home through the streets of Bad News in Newport News, Virginia in his 745 series BMW, he recapped what took place earlier. Then he thought about the four bodies for a quick second. "Shit, it's hard out here right now," he spoke out loud to himself. But then his thoughts drifted off to his two partners, 40 and Block, and how they first met at Hunnington Middle School.

"*Jermaine! Jermaine!*" *he heard as someone was yelled his name. As he turned around to see who it was, he saw nappy-headed Crystal from his homeroom class calling him.*

"*What's up?*" *he said, screwing his face up wondering what the fuck she could want.*

"*Stacy told me to give you this,*" *Crystal said and handed to him a little letter from one of the finest girls in the school. Then she walked away giggling.*

*He was kind of used to all the attention at school with him being the new guy and all. He got kicked out of his last school for fighting too much. Jermaine had only been at this school for one week now.*

*As he opened the letter, he smiled to himself at how he'd just saw her in class smiling so seductively at him. Then he thought she could've given him the letter herself. But you know how girls are at the tender age of thirteen, shy but flirtatious. He started reading the letter.*

*Dear Jermaine,*
*I seen you watching me because I been watching you too and I really like what I am looking at. I just wanted to welcome you to Hunnington Middle School and I hope you like the sights you see, meaning me. If you want to talk, meet me in the band room at lunchtime.*
*Sincerely,*

*Your new friend*

*He closed the letter smiling and tucked it in his pocket. The letter was cool. She's a little feisty and fast, he thought and smiled. Just the way I like them.*

*Come to find out later on, the band room was the spot where couples would meet during lunch. There were no teachers there and it was in the back of the school in the cut. After his third class came to an end, he went to his locker and threw his books in. As he did this, he felt like someone was watching him.*

*When he turned his head to his left, he saw Stacy down the hall looking at him smiling. Then she started to walk down the band hallway. As he saw her leave, he closed his locker and headed in her direction when his stomach growled. He thought, Fuck this bitch. I'm 'bout to go to lunch and eat. It's pizza and French fry day. Then he thought, Naw, I ain't gon' to stand shorty up.*

*As he walked down the hallway and entered the band room, he looked around and saw there were at least ten people in there already. The room was big. There were two guys by the window, smoking weed. He inhaled the smell.*

*"Damn, I love that scent," he said to himself. Everybody else was paired up. Some were talking and some were kissing on each other. As he looked around towards the back, he saw Stacy looking at him with that seductive smile.*

*"What's up?" he said, approaching her.*

*"You," Stacy replied, still smiling.*

*"Oh yeah?" Jermaine said, a little shocked at her semi-intense reply.*

*"Yeah. So where you from?" Stacy asked.*

*"I'm from Downtown, Bad News. Where you think?" he asked, sitting down, looking at her like she was crazy.*

*"Oh, my fault. I'm from 17th. Where you rest at?"*

*"I'm from Marshal Courts, but I stay with my grandma on 42nd street,"* he replied. *"I seen you watching me in class too, like I was your favorite movie or something,"* he said, trying to see that smile again.

*"It takes someone to see someone,"* she replied, blushing.

Jermaine smiled then said, *"You need to wear that more often."*

She looked down and asked, *"What, my skirt?"*

*"Naw, that smile,"* he replied, looking into her eyes. She couldn't help but show all her thirty-twos, smiling harder than ever. As soon as Jermaine asked her if she had a boyfriend, three guys walked in the room and that same smile she wore quickly disappeared.

As they looked around the room, the one in the front spotted who he was looking for and started walking towards her yelling.

*"I was looking for you everywhere and you up in here with some new nigga!"* he yelled, causing a scene for everyone to look on.

As the three stopped in front of them, Jermaine stood up quickly and thought, *Damn, not again. I haven't even been here a full two weeks yet.*

Stacy continued to sit, looking stupid like she had got caught stealing something. Jermaine looked at the guy in front that was doing all the talking, then he looked back at Stacy.

*"I guess my last question answered itself, huh?"* Jermaine said to Stacy.

*"And what was your last question?"* the guy asked, standing in front of the other two like he ran the crew.

Jermaine looked at him and answered, *"Does she have a boyfriend?"*

*"Yes, she does and that's me. So who the fuck is you?"* he asked loudly, so everyone in the room could hear him.

*Jermaine looked at him, then at his two boys that were mugging him, then back at Stacy's so-called boyfriend.*

*"Well, I was gonna be her boyfriend for an hour or two before you came and fucked my groove up."*

*Everyone in the room busted out laughing, including Stacy. Then all of a sudden, Stacy's boyfriend punched Jermaine square in the face. Jermaine stumbled a little, but quickly caught his balance.*

*As Stacy's boyfriend came towards him, Jermaine hit him with a quick and hard two-piece and dropped him. Then his boys rushed him and had him up in the face, kneeling down at the same time. You would've thought he turned into a turtle the way his head was ducked off. Then out of nowhere, he felt the punches stop. As soon as he looked up, he saw the two guys that were smoking by the window come to his aid, beating up the two guys that were on him.*

*After fighting for a couple seconds, he saw Stacy's boyfriend getting up from off the ground. Before he could get up all the way, Jermaine went over, kicked him in the face and dropped him again.*

*As Jermaine began to stomp him, the two guys with him came and pulled him off of Stacy's boyfriend because he was stomping him so bad. Jermaine looked around, breathing heavy and looked at the other two guys on the floor.*

*"A yo, good looking out. But why y'all help me?" Jermaine asked, still breathing heavy.*

*"Shit, you looked like you needed some assistance," the short one said.*

*"We don't fuck with uptown niggas no way," the other one chimed in.*

*Jermaine looked at the three guys that were still on the ground and said, "Let's get outta here." As they walked off, everyone's eyes were on them.*

*"Jermaine," someone called out as they were walking off.*

16

*As he turned around, he saw it was Stacy giving him a piece of paper with her number on it. She had that same smile. He took it and looked at her for a second and walked off. He decided she wouldn't be hearing from him. Girls like her and that smile would get a brother killed. As Jermaine and the two dudes that helped him walked down the hallway, Jermaine asked, "What's y'all names?"*

*"Alvin, but call me Block," the taller one said.*

*"The name is Robert, but don't ever call me that. Everybody calls me 40."*

*"What they call you 40 for?" Jermaine asked, being curious.*

*When he asked him that, 40 looked at Block then back at Jermaine before he glanced down and said, "Because I keep that 40 on me."*

*When he looked down, Jermaine eyes followed and saw the handle of his gun poking through his shirt.*

*"Even in school, huh?" Jermaine asked, looking at him with a smirk on his face.*

*"No doubt," 40 replied with a smile.*

*"My kinda nigga," Jermaine said, dapping up 40.*

*"What's your name or your alias?" Block asked.*

*"Jermaine to the government, but I go by Skalez," Jermaine replied.*

*"What they call you Skalez for?" Block asked him.*

*Jermaine looked at him with a grim smile and said, "It's a long story, but we can fuck with each other for a while and you can find out."*

*"Why they call you Block?" Skalez asked the same question his new friend had just asked him.*

*"They call me Block because I'm always on somebody's block trying to get that paper."*

*"Okay, I can respect that," Skalez said, giving Block some dap.*

*Beep, Beep, Beep!*

Someone behind Skalez blew their horn, shaking him from his thoughts. As he pulled off from the light, he started to reminisce about his crew again. They were grimy when it came to that money and had all type of schemes to get it.

When the three friends got together, it seemed that other niggas' situations and living arrangements got worse. Block and 40 always let Skalez lead the way because he was the thinker out of his crew, especially when it came to getting that fast cash.

The way Skalez and his two-man team was getting money, you would have thought they were some real serious hustlers. But if you knew Skalez, you wouldn't think he was on some stick up shit. With the way he dressed and stayed in the latest fashions, people always called him a pretty boy.

At the age of twenty-three years old, standing at 6'4", weighing 201 pounds with a caramel brown-skinned complexion and corn rolls that slightly hung over his shoulders, he was always a female magnet. But only to the people who didn't know what he did for a living. The ballers, the money getting niggas that ended up in the food chain, were a ready-made meal for him.

Skalez had a lot of love for his boys, 40 and Block. He would hold court in the middle of the streets for his comrades. He got his name Skalez from his older, deceased brother. He always told him if he was going to be out there in those streets, he had to build his weight up and get that paper.

Get so much paper that he couldn't count it all, instead just weighing it on a scale. So, he adopted the name Skalez. He knew the scale that was used to weigh whales was huge, so he knew he had a lot of money to get.

*Ring, Ring.*

Skalez' cell phone went off, breaking his thoughts again. He looked at the screen on his phone. When he saw who it was, he sighed. Then hit the talk button on the phone.

"Speak on it," he answered.

"Where the fuck you been at?" Paula yelled into the phone. He took the phone away from his ear and looked at it like, *Who the fuck this bitch talking to?* Skalez could still hear her fussing through the phone, even after he pulled away from his ear. He put it back up to his ear all calm and cool.

"What's good, baby? Good to hear from you, too."

"Don't 'what's good, baby' me. You forgot we were supposed to go out tonight, huh?"

*Damn, I forgot all about that shit, but money comes first,* Skalez thought.

"Skalez, I know you hear me," Paula said loudly.

"Yeah, I heard you, but something came up and I had to go check on something across the water out in Norfolk."

"What came up?" Paula's attitude was *lit*.

"I'm like five minutes away from the crib. I'll see you when I get there." Skalez then hung up on Paula.

As he parked in front of his town house and got out his car, Paula was in the door waiting on him.

"Why you couldn't just call me to let me know you had different plans?" she asked with her hands on her hips.

"I told you it was urgent. Why you tripping?" Skalez walked past her. "We go out like every other day anyway."

"Ugh, you make me sick sometimes," Paula whined, slamming the door and walking off to the kitchen.

As she walked off mad, Skalez was looking at her in her boy shorts cutting all up in her ass and the tight tee shirt that was hugging her nicely firm C-cups. Paula, standing at 5'4" and weighing 130 pounds was a bombshell. Her skin complexion looked like she been baptized in honey as she kept a year-round glow. You would have thought she was from some type of island, especially with her long, curly hair that came down to the middle of her back. She had a straight hourglass frame. Paula and Skalez met at Norfolk State

University College also known as NSU, where she attended school.

After their first date, they had been riding together ever since. She worked as a nurse at Sentera Hospital. Skalez watched Paula bend over in her boy shorts, getting something out of the refrigerator. He felted his manhood rise. When she shut the door, she turned around to meet Skalez staring at her with lustful eyes.

"Why you looking at me like that?"

"Because you look so cute when you mad and it's something about them boy shorts you wearing right now," Skalez explained, while walking towards her.

She couldn't resist him if she tried to. He always got the best of her. As he pinned her against the refrigerator, he started to plant kisses softly on her neck, giving her shivers.

"Umm. Baby just call next time, ok," Paula said, moaning softly with her eyes closed and head bent back. Skalez didn't reply. He just continued taking her shirt off from over her head. As he started flickering his tongue in between her breast, she stopped him.

"Naw, baby. Let me do this." She knelt down and undid his belt and unbuckled his pants, pulling them down to his knees. "Ain't he happy to see me," Paula said lustfully at his manhood, standing firm and saluting her. Then she took him into her mouth and began to work her magic.

"Damn, baby, that feel so good." Skalez looked down at her. She gently grabbed his balls and started massaging them, while she slobbed and twisted her head in a back and forth motion for a while.

He grabbed the back of her head with both hands. Then she took all of him in her mouth slowly until she reached the base of his dick and his pubic hairs. While doing that, she stuck her tongue out, licking his balls.

*Got damn, she a beast,* he thought.

"I know they didn't teach you that in college," Skalez said. Then all of a sudden, she started sucking his dick with force while looking up at him, her throat feeling like a vacuum. "Ohhh, got damn, Angel. I'm 'bout to cum, baby."

As Skalez's body jerked, she started going faster. When he let his load off in her mouth, she swallowed while slowing down on his dick. After she drained him and got every drop out, she stood up as he took off his pants all the way.

He picked her 5'4" frame up and placed her on the counter. Then he took off her boy shorts. As he knelt down some to get a better view before he started his session of foreplay, she leaned back some. Then he went to work, flickering his tongue on her cunt. She moaned, loving every bit of it because Skalez had a serious tongue game.

He put both of her legs around his neck and really started showing her how his mouthpiece worked. His bottom lip slipped inside her wetness as the top lip was over the clit while his tongue stimulated the clit.

"Mmmm. Ooohh," Paula moaned, grabbing the back of his head. He started giving her pussy French kisses, then stuck his index finger in and around. Then he started waving his finger in her pussy in a "come here" motion.

While slurping on her clit, he hit her G-spot with his finger. She started moaning loudly and breathing heavily, enjoying the pleasurable moments from climaxing.

"I—I—I—I'm cumming, baby. I'm cumming!" As her thighs tightened around his neck, her legs began to shake tremendously.

"Oooh, umm. Don't stop, baby." Her legs were still shaking.

After she let out all of her love juices all over his face, she took her legs from around his neck, letting him breath. Skalez stood up and wiped his mouth and chin.

"Come on, let's go take a shower," he said.

They made it to the shower and started all over, but this time there was penetration. Afterwards, they made it to the bed and lay down, lost in their own thoughts.

"Baby, you got some good ass head." Skalez came out of nowhere and told her.

She smiled. "That's crazy because I was just thinking the same about you." They laughed and talked for a little while before they nodded off.

# Chapter 3

Before Skalez headed out to Tashia's crib, he hit his boys up so they could meet him over there.

"Yo, who this?" 40 answered his phone.

"Damn nigga, you don't check to see who's calling before you pick up your jack?"

"Naw, my nigga. I ain't ducking nobody," 40 replied.

"Yeah a'ight, I got something that uh make your ass duck," Skalez said, goofing around.

"Where you at, fam'? Sounds like you in traffic."

"Yeah, I'm about to head over to Tashia's crib real quick. She said she gotta holla at me about something. Ah look, I need you to call Block and y'all two meet me at her crib in like an hour. Oh yeah, don't forget to bring my break down from last night."

"What time is it?" 40 asked.

"Time for your ass to punch in the clock!" Skalez replied and hung up.

"Yo Skalez!" 40 yelled into the phone. He looked down at the screen of his phone and realized Skalez had hung up. 40 started shaking his head. He looked at his clock on the nightstand and saw it was a little after noon.

"Damn, I must've been tired as shit," he said out loud to himself. Soon as he was about to call Block, he heard the toilet flush in his bathroom down the hallway. "What the fuck!" he said to himself, quickly getting up and grabbing his burner off the nightstand next to the bed. As he crept up on the bathroom, a woman came out. She started screaming when she saw the barrel of a gun in her face.

"What the fuck is your problem?" she yelled mad and scared at the same time.

40 looked at her for a couple of seconds, gun still pinned, then lowered his gun. He forgot he took a stripper home from Magic City last night. He usually didn't take anyone to his

23

crib, damn sure no females knowing how shiesty those New-port News bitches were.

Only Skalez and Block knew where he stayed. He forgot that after him and his boys pulled a caper, he and Block ditched the stolen van, then went back to Magic City off Jefferson Avenue.

"My fault, shorty. I just ain't used to having no company over the crib." She looked at him like he was crazy or something. "What's your name?" he asked, not remembering if he knew.

"Chocolate."

"Ok. I got to make a move real quick, so I'ma call a cab for you."

She sucked her teeth and started walking towards the bedroom to put her clothes on. As she walked by him naked and mad, he looked at her ass jiggling with each stride.

*Oh yeah, I remember last night now,* he thought to himself with a slight grin on his face. He went into the room, placed his gun down and picked up his house phone. He called Porters Cab Service and gave them the directions to his crib while watching her get dressed.

After he hung up the phone, he reached for his pants and pulled out a knot of money. He pulled off two hundred dollars and gave it to her. She started smiling. "Thank you." It was crazy how money could change a person's demeanor.

"So, when I'ma see you again?" She put the money in her purse.

"If the moment's right, it might be tonight," 40 replied, but he knew he wasn't seeing her later on that night.

*Shit, I'ma eligible bachelor. I switch hoes like clothes,* he thought to himself. Ten minutes later, the cab driver was out front, blowing the horn. They said their goodbyes and 40 smacked her on the ass as she left out the front door.

He decided to call Block to tell him Skalez wanted them to meet him at Tashia's crib and about the stripper. After they talked for a couple more minutes, they hung up. 40 then took a shower and got dressed, leaving out the front door of his crib.

He was cruising down Mercury Boulevard in his brand new 2007 Tahoe. Everything was factory except the Kenwood system he had in the back, sounding like two gorillas trying to escape from the trunk. Jay-Z's "Feeling It" off the *Reasonable Doubts* album, was bumping through the speakers.

"I'm feeling it, the high you get from the la," he sang along with the music, while pulling on a blunt in the ashtray. He turned down the volume on the music when his phone rang.

"Yo, who this?"

"This the grim reaper speaking. Nigga, where you at?" Block asked.

"Oh, what's good, playboy? Where you at?" 40 asked, recognizing the voice.

"Me and Skalez already at Tashia's crib."

"A'ight, give me five minutes. I'm on Chestnut now," 40 said and hung up his phone.

As he passed some apartments called Chestnut Arms on his left side, he glanced over and remembered when he and his mom used to stay out there before quickly shaking his thoughts away. When he reached the front of Tashia's apartments on 16th street, he saw Skalez's BMW and Block's Lexus, pulling in and parking behind them.

Grabbing his 40 Ruger off his lap and putting it in his holster, he took the keys out of the ignition and hopped out the truck with his 5'10" frame. As he walked to Tashia's stoop, a feind asked him was he straight. 40 just looked at him and kept it pushing. Approaching the front door, Skalez opened it to let him inside.

"What up, fam'?" he spoke, greeting Skalez.

"Shit, that work. Now that's what's up," Skalez replied, shutting the door after 40 entered the apartment.

"I got it in the truck. Damn, you sweating a nigga like a baby mother trying to get child support. But what's up with y'all?" He looked at Block.

"Boy, your ass was tricking hard as shit last night," said Block.

"Fuck you talking about?" 40 asked before he took a seat.

"Shit, the way you were throwing money on all them hoes in Magic City last night made me wanna start dancing! You changed the forecast from hot and sunny, 90-degree weather to a thunderstorm out in South Africa." Block laughed.

"Nigga, you don't even know where South Africa at and I know your ass ain't talking. I saw your ass in the corner with that bunny tricking like it was the first of April."

"Yeah, snow bunny had me gone. I ain't gon' lie. I ain't never seen no white girl with an ass like that," Block said, thinking about the stripper.

"You fucking with them salty, Wonder Bread ass bitches now?" Skalez interjected.

"Damn, you said that shit like you racist or something."

"Nigga, how the fuck can I be racist when I got a pocket full of dead white people." Skalez pulled out a big cartoon knot of money out of both of his pockets. "Speaking of money, do you got my 12 zips?" Skalez asked, turning his head to 40.

"I told your amnesia having ass I got it in the truck," 40 replied. As soon as 40 said that, Tashia strolled in from the back of the apartment, looking like a young version of Buffy the Body. At the age of 21, she had two bad ass sons, but her body didn't show it at all, having no stretch marks from pregnancy.

She was always wearing shirts that showed off her flat stomach and her belly button ring. Her breasts were a size D-cup and she was 43 inches in the ass. Standing at 5'10", she was a straight stallion. Her skin complexion was in between a Hershey Bar and a caramel sundae and she looked really tasty on a bad day. Tashia was like part of the family, sort of. She was used for bait to catch some of the big fish niggas that were making paper.

"What y'all crazy niggas yelling 'bout in here?" Tashia asked, coming in swinging her hips, but not trying to, in her tight, low rider Apple Bottom Jeans.

"Ain't shit. We just tripping about some bullshit," Skalez told her.

"A'ight, listen up, fellas," Tashia said, sitting down next to Skalez. "Y'all remember that guy Lance I put y'all up on last week, right?"

"Well, check this out," Tashia said without even waiting for a response. "He took me out last night to Cheesecake Factory out in Norfolk on Waterside Drive by MacArthur Mall. But before we went there, he said he had to make a stop somewhere. So y'all know a bitch like me ain't gonna ask no questions about where we going or nothing to raise antennas, so I said 'ok, no problem'. But to make a long story short—"

"Hold up! Hold up! Fuck that!" Skalez said, cutting her off, "If it's about money, make a short story long!"

"No bullshit,"40 added.

"Listen to you niggas, like this is a bitch first time doing this shit," Tashia said. "Let me tell you my 'about to get money' story," she said, grinning.

"So, like I was saying before I was rudely interrupted, we stopped at a house that looked like it was not being used. Grass needed cutting and all, but he left me in the car for like ten minutes. Then when he came out the house, he had a brown paper bag in his hand. I played it off and paid it no mind, didn't even ask what was in the bag. When he got in the car, he placed it in the back seat on the floor and we drove to the Cheesecake Factory."

"Hold up one more time," Skalez interjected. "Do you even remember where the house is?"

"Nigga, you know I got photographic memory. We got off on exit 1013, went down Church Creek and made a left on West Avenue. Then we stopped at house 1135," she replied quickly, while Skalez just smiled at her.

"Yeah, you on your shit," Block said, smiling at her.

"She better be if she wants to get paid," Skalez said seriously, looking at her.

"But anyway, like I was saying," Tashia started again, "When we was at our table, I just started going through my purse like I was looking for something. He asked me what I was looking for, so I told him my phone and that I must've left it in the car. I told him I needed it just in case the babysitter called about my sons and that anything can happen. So, the dumb ass nigga handed me the keys to his Benz. I told the waiter what I wanted, then headed out the door. Before I opened the car door, I looked to see if he could see me from the restaurant, but he couldn't because of where he was sitting. After I got my phone off the floor I dropped before we got out the car, I reached in the back on the floor and looked inside the bag. Just as a bitch expected, it was full of money. I closed it back, locked the door and went back inside the restaurant."

"Jackpot," Skalez said, smiling.

"You been dealing with Lance for a month now, right?" 40 asked Tashia.

"Yeah, about that."

"And this nigga ain't take you to his crib or nothing yet?"

"That nigga Lance is an extra scary nigga. Plus, I been acting like I don't want to give up the goods on some hard to get shit," Tashia disclosed. "Then he always looking in the mirror on some paranoid shit."

"Naw, that nigga just being extra careful, trying to duck them laws," said 40.

"Yeah, and duck niggas like us," Skalez added, with an evil look on his face. "But check this out." He rubbed his hands together. "We gonna watch this nigga for a couple of days to see what we stumble on before we make a move. We need you to find out where this nigga stay and Tashia we need you to stay on point and turn it up a little because we know this nigga got more at his crib somewhere. We gonna jack that nigga for every dime he got. He been getting a lot of money down here in the city for a long time. What time you supposed to see that nigga again?"

"He said he was going to call me today," Tashia replied, looking at Skalez sitting beside her.

"A'ight, look. The next time he calls, hit me up right afterwards and let me know the 411 like if he wants to get up with you. If he does, that's when the tag game comes into play."

"Ah look, I'm 'bout to roll out and get me something to eat. Nigga stomach emptier than a broke nigga's pockets." 40 rubbed his stomach as he stood up.

"Yeah, before your ass go, drop them joints off in my car. As a matter of fact, I'm about to roll out, too," Skalez told them.

"Me, too," Block replied, jumping to his feet with his chain swinging from his neck.

"Hey, before y'all go, I need a couple of dollars to do something around the house," Tashia lied, knowing she was going to get her nails done.

"I knew you wasn't going to let us make it," 40 said, laughing and reaching in his pockets.

They all broke her off with a couple bills while heading to the door. She complimented Block on his chain. Skalez and 40 just looked at Block, then left out the door.

# Chapter 4

Lance was a bonafide hustler from up top. He was originally from Harlem, New York, but had been down in Virginia for the last few years making some serious paper. It's why he was there, knowing there wasn't anything but money throughout the cities in the Tide Water area. He began to like the area and made it his home.

He had a mini mansion built in Smithfield County, in a little country area of Virginia away from the city parts. He was comfortable in his surroundings, but was more concerned about the money then anything else. So no one knew where he lived. His motto was 'never shit where you lay,' not even in the city you lived in.

Lance had been thinking about this girl he'd been dealing with for the last month. *It's like she playing hard to get, but I'm down for the chase,* he thought to himself. He couldn't shake the way her ass was looking in that mini skirt she had on yesterday when they went out.

"Damn, how she got all that ass in that little skirt?" he asked himself. Then he thought back to how they first met at this place called The Alley, out in Newport News.

Lance shook the thought and dialed a number in his phone. He turned the music down in his S550 Benz while driving through the city.

"Hello," Tashia answered.

"How you doing, sexy?"

"Better now, hearing your voice."

"Oh yeah? Well the feeling is mutual."

"I really didn't think I was going to hear from you today. Where you at?" Tashia asked.

"I'm out in Norfolk right now for a minute. Why, what's up?"

"Ain't nothing. I just wanted to see you sometime today, that's all."

"Well, we can definitely arrange that. Just let me handle this business and I'll call you when I'm on my way, a'ight?"

"Okay, sweetie," Tashia said in a soft sexy tone.

"A'ight. One." Lance hung up, smiling to himself.

Pulling up to his destination, he turned the car off and grabbed the book bag that was on the passenger seat and got out. As he entered the house, he threw the bag on the couch a couple of feet away, then shut and locked the door. He went into the kitchen and grabbed him a Corona beer out the refrigerator, popped the top and took a sip while walking back to the living room. His cell phone started to ring. He stopped and took his phone off his hip and looked at the screen.

"Yeah, speak on it."

"What's good, L?" the guy said.

"You already know, playboy. Let me know something."

"I'm ready."

"Same thing?"

"Naw, the baby ran out of food too fast the last time. You might wanna bring an extra box," the guy implied.

"Yeah, you right! Can't let the babies go hungry. Give me about 30 minutes."

"Alright," the guy replied and hung up.

Lance walked over to the couch, putting his phone back in the clip. He picked up the bag and headed to the back room. When he made his way to the bed, he stopped at the side of it, then flipped the mattresses and box spring off it, leaning against the wall.

He stepped inside the bed rails and knelt down where there was a cut in the carpet, pulling it back at the seam. Next, he took the top piece of the floor that was cut out and started turning the knob on his safe.

"Seven to the left, 29 to the right, and 4 back to the left," he said out loud to himself.

When the safe door clicked and opened, he was all smiles. He smiled every time he looked at his cash. He opened the book bag, then started placing money stacks on top of money stacks in the safe. He had $250,000 in there. After he placed everything back in order, he went into the kitchen, opened the big deep freezer and moved some items from the top. Reaching to the bottom, he pulled out three ice cream boxes and placed them in the same book bag he just had the money. Then he placed the items he moved back on top and closed the deep freezer. That's where Lance kept his work, in the deep freezer. But he rigged it so the temperature was just a little bit below refrigerator temperature, allowing him to put certain foods in the deep freezer.

While leaving out the house and walking towards his Benz, he remembered looking at Tashia yesterday when he brought her over there and left her in the car. *Damn, little momma look good,* he thought. As he was driving down Church Street, he looked at the time. It read 6:15.

"I can be to her by seven," he said to himself, picking his cell phone up to call Tashia.

"What's going on, sweetie?" Tashia answered.

"How you know it was me?" Lance asked.

"Caller I.D., baby," she said with a little laugh.

"Oh yeah! That's right, but check this out. Be ready to go around seven."

"Where we going?" Tashia asked.

"I'm leaving that up to you."

"I know where we can go," she said in a sexy tone.

"Where?"

"To Mars," she replied.

"What the fuck is that? A new club or something?" Lance asked, not knowing.

"Naw, baby. That's how high you're going to feel when you up in me," she cooed.

"Oh yeah? Well what time is lift off?" Lance asked, grinning. "We gotta get something to eat first because a brother hungry. I haven't eaten since earlier this morning."

"You too! I haven't eaten since earlier myself."

"Ah look, I'ma call you when I'm in Newport News."

"All right, baby." Tashia disconnected.

Lance put his cell phone down on his lap. *I'ma turn her ass into a porn star tonight.*

# Chapter 5

The phone rang a time or two before Skalez answered it. "Talk to me," he said, in an even tone.

"Hello to you, too," Tashia said back.

"Tell me something good."

"Well, I just got off the phone with him a second ago. He 'bout to come scoop me up in like 40 minutes."

"That's good. Now look, you gotta work your magic on this nigga. Hopefully, he'll take you to the crib since you haven't been intimate with him yet."

"Boy, if y'all don't stop throwing that got damn football near my house, I'ma break my foot off in y'all asses," she said before responding to Skalez's last comment. "I just had his ass open like an all-night boot leg house on the phone."

"Cool," Skalez said.

"What happens if he takes me to a hotel room?"

"I know. I was thinking the same thing."

"You crazy ass niggas just ain't gonna bust up in there why I'm in there, are you?"

"Hell naw. I told you we only following this nigga for now to see his whereabouts."

"Good, 'cause I ain't trying to be around you crazy ass niggas when y'all get him," Tashia said, knowing how them niggas got down.

"Yeah, whatever. We just need to know where this nigga lays his head. We gon' be tailing y'all tonight!"

"What kind of ride y'all going to be in?" Tashia asked.

"You worried about all the wrong things. Just do your part, baby girl." Skalez hung up, then turned to look at his partners in crime, 40 and Block. "That was Tashia right there. Our boy coming out to play tonight."

\*\*\*

"Damn, Tink. You gonna charge a nigga like that for this rusty piece of shit?" 40 asked the crackhead.

"Hey man, you know it's fucked up out here. How you get out here anyway?" Crackhead Tink asked.

"Nigga, I walked with your nosey ass. But look, I'ma give you that because I need the car all night. But if you tell someone I got your car, I mean anyone, I'ma blow this bitch up with your ass in it."

"Come on, 40. You know I ain't with that. I just wanna get high, man. I need a fix bad as shit." Tink scratched his face.

"You need a fix, huh? So does your teeth and your motherfucking breath, nigga. Back up breath, smelling like crab meat and shit," 40 said, squinching his face up from the smell of his breath. "Here, take this shit. I'ma see you in the morning." 40 rolled out in the friend's car.

As he turned the corner on 41st street, he saw Block and Skalez waiting inside Skalez's Beamer. He pulled up beside them, then rolled the window down.

"I'ma go park my car a block away from Tashia's spot. Just follow me," Skalez said and pulled off. Looking at his watch, he had twelve minutes to seven. *It will take 5 minutes to get her crib*, Skalez thought to himself.

Stopping at the light, two females blew their horn in a Honda Civic next to them. Skalez paid them no mind, but Block, on the other hand, rolled down his window to holla at the two cuties.

"What's good with you two ladies?" Block asked through the passenger side window.

"Ain't nothing. Just trying to find something to get into," the driver replied out the window.

"Oh yeah? Well I see something I'm trying to get into right now."

"What's good with your man behind the wheel?" the other chick in the Honda asked.

As soon as she said that, the light turned green and Skalez drove off like they weren't even there.

"What you doing? You ain't trying to get at them hoes? Them bitches trying to fuck," Block said excitedly, looking at Skalez.

"Fam, I don't have no time to be chasing no bitches. I'm steady chasing paper. Shit, we literally chasing some right now. Besides that, them sack chasing bitches, Katrina and Trish from Newsome Park. Shit, they chasing paper, too," Skalez said, putting emphasis on his last words.

"Man, that was Trish? I heard that bitch can do all type of tricks on a dick," Block said, then sighed.

"Fuck that bitch. You know I'm with you definitely on this paper chasing shit, but nigga, I like to fuck, too. You know our motto, 'Money over bitches'," Block and Skalez both said at the same time.

They pulled over and parked on the side of Magruder Elementary School around the corner from Tashia's apartment. Skalez and Block hopped out the Beamer and got in the old Buick Regal with 40. As they parked seven cars down from Tashia's crib, Skalez said it was seven o'clock on the dot. As soon as he said that, 40 pointed. "There go that nigga's Benz right there."

As Lance was pulling up to Tashia's apartment, he started dialing her number.

"Hey, you," Tashia said, answering.

"I'm out front. Come on," Lance advised her.

"Alright, let me grab my purse and phone," she replied, while disconnecting the call.

When she walked down the walkway, Lance couldn't do anything, but stare at the stallion beauty. Her jeans looked like they were air brushed on. He started grinning when she approached the car and got in.

"What's good, sexy?" He leaned over to kiss her on the cheek.

"Nothing, just glad to be in your presence again," she replied with a smile, showing her dimples.

"So, tell me where we are headed?"

"I was thinking Olive Garden."

"That's a good choice. I like eating their Chicken Alfredo."

Tailing them, the crew was beamed in.

"Look at this nigga getting out of his car looking like a fat Gerald Lavert," Block said about Lance.

"Shit, the nigga eating good," Skalez replied back.

"No bullshit. You see them Ashanti Rims he sitting on. I might have to buy me a set for my truck or just take his. What you think?"

"They're sweet."

"Here, you wanna hit this?" 40 asked, trying to pass the blunt to Skalez.

"Naw, I'm focused, fam."

"Man, shit! This help a nigga like me focus. Pass that shit back here," Block said, reaching for the bunt.

"I wonder how long they gonna be up in Olive Garden," 40 said, getting worried.

"Until they done eating, fool," Block said, coughing on the weed.

"Man, gimme my shit back. You can't even handle purp," 40 chuckled, turning around reaching for the blunt. "You sporting that chain, too. Them diamond cuts and two rubies gushing under that light," 40 said, grabbing the blunt and looking at the chain around Block's neck.

"Yeah, you like it, huh?" Block replied.

"Shit, you need to get rid of that shit. Sell it or something. It look like he got that shit custom made," Skalez said seriously.

"Yeah, custom made for me," Block replied with a smile on his face.

"Anyway, we need to focus on this nigga. Fuck that chain. You doing a good job tailing him too, 40. You're not too close or too far. You blending in good with the traffic," Skalez said to 40, switching the topic from the chain.

\*\*\*

"Welcome to Olive Garden. My name is Tracy and I am going to be your waiter for tonight. Would you like to order now?" the waiter asked.

"Umm, yes. I will take the Chicken Parmesan dish with a side of a Chicken Caesar salad with no dressing," Tashia said, already knowing what she wanted.

"And for you, sir?" the waiter asked.

"I guess I'll take the Shrimp Fettuccini meal and a chicken salad, also," Lance said, putting down the menu.

"Anything to drink?"

"Yes, we will take a bottle of Grey Goose and two glasses of apple juice."

"Excellent choice. I'll be back with your meal shortly." The waiter smiled, and then walked off.

"What's the apple juice for?" Tashia asked.

"Just in case you need a chaser," Lance replied. "Oh, and honey, you looking really delicious tonight."

"Thank you! You don't look too bad yourself." Tashia smiled.

"Are you able you stay out and play tonight for a while?"

"Baby, I'm grown! The only curfew I got is to not be late when your light pole turn on."

"I'm feeling that right there, but I was talking about your kids. Do you have to return home tonight?"

"Oh no, sweetie. The babysitter got them for tonight, so it's good for us to make a movie."

Lance liked what he was hearing. She just came out of nowhere with all this freaky shit recently. He thought she might be coming around, thinking it was time to give up the goodies.

After they ate at Olive Garden, it was a little after nine o'clock. As they were cruising down Mercury Boulevard, he made a left turn on Coliseum Drive, then made a quick left into the Shell gas station. When he parked his Benz, he got out.

"You want something from out of here?" Lance asked.

"No, I'm okay. Thank you," Tashia replied.

"All right." He shut the door.

As he walked to the entrance of the store, he noticed a car pulling in. *Damn, them niggas need to burn that dusty ass car,* he thought and went in the store.

Approaching the cash register, he asked for a pack of Dutch Masters and a pack of Trojan condoms. As the cashier rang his items up, he pulled his cash out and paid for the items, then headed out the door. Pocketing the condoms and walking with the pack of blunts in his hands, he got in the car, put it in gear and drove off.

As he turned onto Coliseum Drive making a left, he saw that beat up ass car again, turning the same direction through his rear view mirror. He paid it no mind and kept going through the yellow light. While pulling into the Embassy Hotel and parking, Tashia's cell phone began to ring.

"Hello."

"You have a long night ahead of you," Skalez said.

"Yeah, I'ma be out all night, so just give the boys a kiss for me and thank you again for watching them on such short notice," Tashia replied, playing it off.

"Alright, just check in with me in the morning."

"Alright, goodbye," Tashia said and hung up.

"The babysitter checking in, huh?" Lance asked.

"Yeah, the babysitter is my girl. She be coming through for me from time to time."

"I dig that!"

\*\*\*

"Well, I guess we ain't gone find out where this nigga stay at tonight." 40 sighed, feeling like they wasted their time.

"Naw, it's cool. It will come. We got the bait with the line out there now and when he bites, that's when we'll reel his ass in," Skalez said, rubbing his hands together.

"Let's roll out and get a couple of drinks. Applebee's right down the street," Block said.

"Man, I ain't trying to get seen in this fiend ass car no more than I have to. You seen all the funny ass stares we got. Fuck that!" 40 replied to Block's suggestion.

"Yeah, drop me off to get my ride," Skalez said.

As they exited the hotel parking lot, they drove back down town to Newsport News. Approaching Skalez's Beamer, Block asked, "What y'all doing for tonight?"

"Shit, I'ma take this pipe head back his raggedy ass car before this breaks down and I end up walking," 40 quipped.

"No bullshit," Skalez agreed.

"We might need this joint tomorrow, too," 40 implied.

"I know. I was just thinking the same thing." Block said.

"I really over paid that dumb ass nigga for this piece of shit. He think I'm bringing it to him in the morning anyway," 40 told them.

"Oh yeah? Well y'all trying to pull a stake out on this nigga until the morning?" Skalez suggested.

"For real, for real! I gotta handle something in a little while," Block said, really trying to meet up with the white stripper he met at Magic City the night before.

"What you gotta handle? It ain't like this money we trying to get," Skalez said, turning his head looking at Block.

"Yeah, you right. It ain't nothing like money," Block said, washing his thoughts away about the stripper.

"We gotta get something to eat first. That weed got a brother hungry than a muthafucker," 40 said.

"Yeah, we gotta do that before we get back on our stake-out shit," Block added.

"Nigga, we jack boys. That's what true jackers do. Time to get this money. Put this raggedy shit in gear and let's roll out." Skalez was hyped up.

"Nigga, you serious bout this shit," 40 said, looking over at Skalez, while pulling off.

"It's only three things that get me serious and aroused. That's my bitch, beef and that mu'fucking paper."

\*\*\*

"Damn, Tashia. You sure know what you know," Lance said, breathing heavy, exhausted from their third round of sex and the way Tashia had put it on him.

"I know a little something," Tashia replied, laying next to Lance.

"I swear I could've stayed inside of you all night," Lance said in a low voice lying on top of the sheets. When I was in you, it felt like I was in a swimming pool skinny dipping for real!

"If it felt like that down there, you damn sure drained it tonight," Tashia said not really meaning it. She was really thinking, *This nigga can't fuck with his little dick. The only thing he can work it is with his tongue and shit. I had to ride that!*

"Yeah baby, you worked over time tonight," Tashia told him as she placed her head on his chest, boosting up his ego.

As they started to doze off, they were interrupted by a phone call.

Lance looked around, knowing the familiar ring as he reached on the nightstand for his phone.

"Yeah," Lance said, answering his phone.

"Ah look, I'm 'bout to head down to Florida for a couple of days. So, you want your money now or when I get back?" the guy spoke into the phone.

"What the fuck is that? A trick question or something?" You know I need mine ASAP," Lance replied, knowing the voice.

"I figured you would say that. Where you wanna meet at?"

"Damn nigga, you 'bout to leave tonight?"

"Yeah, I told you I—"

"What time is it?" Lance said, cutting him off.

"2:45," the guy answered with a shaky voice.

"Damn nigga, you call me at 2:45 in the goddamn morning? Why you didn't call me earlier?" Lance asked aggressively, knowing when money calls, he was going to get it no matter what time it was.

"I know, my fault, but it just came up. Some personal shit. I got to go handle this situation down there. I didn't want you to think I was on some bullshit about yo' money."

"Where you at now?" Lance asked him.

"I'm going through the tunnel out in Hampton headed to Norfolk to pick something up."

"Damn, I wish you would've called before you went out that way. I'm out Hampton right now."

"Damn nigga, you be everywhere."

"Yeah, everywhere you don't be. How long you gonna be out in Norfolk?"

"Like 15 minutes."

"A'ight, meet me at the apartments in front of Hampton University in the parking lot in 45 minutes. You know where that is, right?" Lance asked.

"Yeah, behind Burger King."

"A'ight, I'll see you then," Lance said and disconnected the call.

"Damn!" Lance said, sighing as he looked over he saw Tashia getting dressed.

He was so caught up in his phone call that he didn't even realize that she had gotten out of the bed and was putting her clothes.

"You not mad, are you?" Lance asked, looking at her, while still laying in the bed.

"Naw, not even! Believe me, baby, when the money calls, you have got to go get it," Tashia said, putting emphasis on the words 'money calls'. "I understand how it goes."

*Damn*, he thought. *I might make shorty my little broad. She understands the hustle, the late-night calls and all.*

"You don't want to stay here for tonight?" Lance asked.

"Naw, I might as well get back home to my little men," she replied about her sons.

*That's cool too, because I don't like riding around with that much cash on me no way*, Lance thought.

After they got dressed, they headed out the hotel to his car. He hit the button on his key chain, unlocking the doors and starting his car up.

"So, when I"ma see you again?" Tashia asked after they got in the car.

"Well, with it being Friday at three in the morning, we might can arrange something for tonight. I gotta head out to Richmond tonight for a minute, but on my way back I can definitely make some time to see my lady."

"Oh, I'm you lady now? So I stepped it up from your little baby to your lady?" Tashia asked, blushing.

"Naw, you always going to be my baby, but as of right now, I'm making you my lady," Lance said, smiling at her and pulling off.

"I'm loving the way that sounds," Tashia replied, smiling.

"You got me tired right now," Lance said, yawning. "After I drop you off at home, I'ma go get this money and head to the crib."

Jibril Williams

# Chapter 6

"Yeah, this some good tree right here," 40 said, inhaling the weed.

"Man, Paula blowing the shit out of my phone." Skalez looked at his vibrating phone. "It's three o'clock in the morning and she up calling me. I told her ass I was gon' to be out tonight on our way back over here."

"Yo, Skalez. You know how them females are. That's why I'ma a bachelor. I ain't trying to go through that shit and answer to no female. I do what the fuck I does," Block said from the back seat.

"Hey, hey! Look at what the cat brought out!" 40 announced. With three heads turning towards the entrance of the Embassy Hotel, they spotted Lance and Tashia coming out.

"This shit turning out better than a nigga expected," Skalez said out loud.

Block was pleased. "I'm really glad we don't have to wait until the morning. They might've came out around check out time. That's around 11 or 12 o'clock."

"Ayo, 40. Stay as far back from them as you can. Ain't too many people gon' to be on the road this early," Skalez warned.

40 started the car up and eased out at a nice distant behind them. Trailing them for a while, they knew they were headed back down town to Tashia's apartment on 16$^{th}$ street. As they saw Lance's Benz pull over, they pulled over a block away, watching.

"They must be about to go in her spot," 40 surmised.

"Naw, if they wanted to chill, they would've stayed at the hotel. He 'bout to drop her off," Skalez guessed correctly.

No later than a minute after he said that, they saw Tashia emerge from the vehicle and walk towards her apartment.

After she went in and closed the door, they saw his Benz pull off.

As they followed Lance from a good distance away, they saw him make a right turn on Jefferson Avenue. Following him for a bock and a half, they noticed he put on his left blinker as he turned to get on to the interstate.

"Damn, this nigga getting on the interstate," 40 spoke.

"It don't matter, follow the money," Skalez said, watching the Benz. "We gonna find out where this nigga lay his head at tonight."

They got on the interstate pursuing their prey until they saw him getting off the Hampton University exit. Lance made a right, driving down a half a mile, then made a left into some apartments by the University and parked.

"Damn, I know this nigga don't live out here in no apartments," said 40.

"Might be one of his little spots or one of his girls' crib," guessed Block. Then they saw a car's headlights flash twice.

"I'm 10 minutes late and this nigga still ain't here," Lance spoke to himself before he saw a car blink its headlights twice from across the parking lot. Then Tony got out the car with a bag.

"Damn nigga, I thought your ass wasn't even here yet when I didn't see your Impala," Lance said, getting out his car and shutting the door.

"Naw, I got this rental right here. I told you I'm 'bout to head down south real quick," Tony replied, passing the bag full of money over to Lance.

"It's all here?"

"Every single dollar."

"I don't have to count this shit, do I?" Lance asked, unzipping the bag to look at the cash he knew damn well he wasn't about to count it.

"Come on, big homie. Why you wanna play me like that? You know I ain't never came up short with your shit. Man,

I'll fuck with my momma money before I fuck with yo' shit," Tony said, laughing as he mocked Chris Tucker from the Friday movie.

"Man, you wild, son." Lance laughed as he zipped the bag back up.

"Naw, I'm fucking with you. I know you good, son."

"Why all y'all New York cats be with all that 'son' shit?"

"But I don't call you son cause you mine. I call you son cause you shine." Lance grinned.

"Yeah a'ight, fam."

"Ah look, I'm 'bout to get outta here. Be safe on that interstate, son." Lance dapped Tony up before they departed ways.

Tony got in his rental car and made a right while Lance made a left in the direction he came from. Driving a little further, Tony saw some car's lights turn on and drove passed it.

*Damn, them niggas look like they up to no good this early in the morning in that raggedy ass car*, Tony said to himself, but he kept going.

***

"A yo, you seen that nigga pass him that bag?" Block asked from the back seat.

"It got to be one of the two things," Skalez said, knowing what could be inside the bag.

"I'm going with this one. It's gotta be some money," 40 spoke up.

"We should run up on both them niggas right now and get what's—"

Skalez cut Block off in midsentence. "Easy, cowboy. We want the big shit, not the small shit. And besides, we gonna get that, too. It's going right to his stash which is going directly in our pockets," Skalez said with a slight grin.

"A'ight, they leaving now," observed 40.

"That's good. Lance went the other way," said Block, not wanting to be noticed.

"Damn, you seen the way that other nigga was looking all up in the car as he drove by?" Skalez asked as the guy that met Lance passed them.

"Yeah, he probably looking at how fucked up this car is and wondering how a nigga can drive this shit." 40 then pulled off.

As they started following Lance again, they noticed he didn't get back on Mercury Boulevard, passing Olive Garden, then the Coliseum Mall.

"I wonder where the fuck this nigga going at 4 o'clock in the morning? What the fuck! This nigga live on the road," 40 huffed, sounding sarcastic, but he was serious.

When he passed Jefferson Avenue, they were going over a little overpath and were now passing Warick Boulevard.

"Damn, this nigga going over the James River Bridge headed to Smithfield," Block said. "Man, this nigga taking us all in the country and shit. I'm glad we put gas in this hoopty 'cause this nigga taking us on a roller coaster ride, for real."

"Yeah, that's good," Skalez said.

"Why you say that?" 40 asked.

"Just think about it. It's four in the morning and he going away from the city with a bag of money and his stash house is in Norfolk, which is another city, but we headed to Smithfield County. It's one of the two things," Skalez offered.

"I'm going with number one again. It got to be his crib," 40 said, knowing where Skalez was going with it.

Going over the bridge, they passed by a Race Trac gas station on the right of them. About two miles away and a few turns later, they saw him pull into a long driveway. As they kept going, they passed his house.

"Jackpot." Skalez grin.

"There it goes again," 40 said. "That big ass, Ronald McDonald smile."

"Shit, I even see that shit from the back seat. Your cheeks lifted your whole face up, making your eyes squint like as Asian and shit," Block chimed in, laughing with 40 jumping in. Skalez couldn't help but laugh, too.

"But I only smile like that when I see and get that money or when I got my prey boxed in where I want him," Skalez said.

"Aye 40, you one helluva driver too, fam, for real. I'm glad we on the same team," Block said.

"Now I see how these Feds and detectives be following and building cases up on a nigga all day," Skalez told them. "These niggas need to be more cautious of their surroundings."

"Did you see that nigga's mini mansion? Look like some shit off *MTV Cribs*," Block asked them.

"Yeah, we might have to drive a U-haul truck when we come back and get this nigga," 40 said seriously.

"Turn this piece of shit around and let's go home and get some sleep. Now, all we got to do is put a plan together, then put it in motion," Skalez said.

# Chapter 7

Block sat up, looking at the clock on the dresser to check the time.

"Damn, I gotta get up. What time is it?" he asked himself, looking at the time. *Shit, its 1:30 in the afternoon. Well, I didn't get home until a little after five in the morning following that nigga,* he thought.

As he was getting up, he grabbed the remote and turned on the T.V. Flipping through the channels, he stopped on the news. After watching that for a couple of minutes, he heard them talking about the weather. He started to walk off until what the new reporter said next got his attention

*"This is breaking news from Channel 10 on your side. This is reporter, Christor Wiltkins, reporting live from a house on Carwford Street down the street from Newport News Park. They have found four bodies in a house. It looks like a drug-related robbery that turned into a homicide. They have yet to find a witness or the people who may have done this. If you have anything you know related to this situation, please call 1-800-LOCK-U-UP. That's all for now. Back to you, Steve."*

"Damn, they just now finding them niggas? That shit was a couple days ago, but that's a good thing," Block said to himself and smiled, getting up to take a shower.

Block stayed in York Town County off Durby Bun in the cut. The only people that knew where he stayed were Skalez and 40. His mother knew, but it's like she didn't because he rarely saw her. He loved the hood. Bad News was his stomping grounds and those streets birthed him. But he had done and still was doing too much dirt to continue staying over there. And there were too many niggas knew him and his crew.

They all left from downtown Newport News, him and his boys around the same time after they hit their first lick. They were at the age of 17. Block got his first spot in his uncle's name, but when he came of age, he moved and put everything in his own name. His uncle had his own landscaping business, so he always faked like he had a job.

Now at the age of 22, he was getting that fast money the fast way and the ski mask way and no one could tell him shit. Him and his boys were the only ones their age in the city getting money. So that meant everyone was for grabs and their circle was only a three-man team.

After Block got himself together, he was about to walk out the door until he realized he forgot something.

*Oh yeah,* he thought, turning around going towards the couch in the living room. *Can't leave home without this.* He lifted one of the cushions on the couch, and grabbed his p89 Ruger, putting it on his hip.

Heading out the door, he approached his Lexus and stopped, looking at himself in the tinted windows.

"Damn, a nigga couldn't pay for these looks," he said, pulling his chain out from inside his shirt.

*Ring, Ring, Ring!*

His cell phone started going off.

"Talk to me, I'll talk back."

"Hey, daddy. What's good with you?" the girl said.

"Who this?" Block asked, then looked at the number on the screen.

"This Christy, the girl you met at Magic City the other night."

"Oh yeah, my fault. What's good with you?" He remembered the white stripper with the fat ass.

"Just calling to see what you up to. What you got planned for today?"

"I'm bout to head to the car wash and spray this car down," he said, getting into his car.

"I thought we were gone get up with each other last night. What happened?"

"Yeah, yeah, I know. Some important shit came up that I had to tend to." He drove off from in front of his crib.

"Oh yeah? Well, if I would've seen you last night, somethings would've came up, also. At least two things I can think off," Christy told him slowly and seductively.

"Umm, I like the way you said that."

"What car wash are you going to?"

"The Soap and Suds on Mercury Boulevard."

"You talking about the one across from the Race Trac gas station?"

"Bingo. Why, what's up?" Block asked.

"I just wanted to see your face before I headed out to Virginia Beach."

"Where are you now? I'm out on Fox Hill right now, but I can meet you there."

"A'ight. I'ma be there in fifteen minutes. How long you gon' be?" she asked.

"That's cool, not long. Just look for a midnight black Lexus."

"Ok, daddy."

"Damn, say that again."

"Ha, ha, ha. Ok, daddy," she said, dragging the words.

"A'ight, I'll see you there," Block said, then disconnected the call.

\*\*\*

Pulling up in the car wash with all four windows halfway down, heads were turning as Lil Wayne's "My Leather So Soft" could be heard coming from his speakers.

*My top so soft,*
*I probably have it off*
*These niggas so soft, man,*
*I go so hard bitch*

*I go so hard.*

"That's my shit," someone yelled, rapping along with the song.

As he passed people at a slow creep, they were nodding their head to the music like the speakers was actually speaking to them. He pulled into one of the open spaces to wash his car and hopped out his Lex. His chain swung with the music still playing while walking to the change machine.

Females were gawking him. Even the ones with their man were stealing glances at him. He paid it no mind because he was used to the attention, especially when him and his boys were out. Making his way back to his car, he put two dollars worth of quarters in and started rinsing his car down before sudding it up with soap.

He was washing his rims off when he heard a horn beep from behind him. He turned his head quickly to see who it was. When Christy got out of her Ford Explorer truck, Block just stared like he was caught in a trance.

She had on a tight white Gucci tee that had the two Gs on the front with some tight white shorts with the brown and white Gucci belt to hold it up. But really it was her ass that held it all up. The belt was just for show and coordination.

The white 4-inch heels complemented her thighs and ass. With all that white on, she would've given Lisa Raye a run for her money. *Damn, look at that camel toe between them legs*, Block said to himself.

Christy wasn't your average white girl. She was like CoCo, the model, with her 5'5" frame, long blonde hair and ass that looked like you could sit a 40-ounce bottle on it. Yeah, she just that swole.

"Damn baby, pick your mouth up," Christy said with a smile.

"You looking like vanilla ice cream right now, really tasty like," Block said, grinning.

"You act right, you might get a taste. Now come over here and give me a hug."

As he dropped the water pressure hose, he went over and gave her a tight hug while squeezing her ass.

"You just couldn't resist it, huh?"

He could tell she wanted a kiss, but he wasn't the kissing type of nigga, let alone her being a stripper. If he kissed her, then he might as well kiss the whole city.

"You gonna help me finish washing my car?"

"Am I getting paid?" she asked, putting her hand on her hip like she was about to rip the runway.

"Yeah, with gratitude and being blessed by my presence." Block was acting real nonchalant.

"Well, seeing you is worth enough for right now." She walked passed him to pick up the water pressure hose.

Bending over to pick it up, she turned to see if he was watching. She smiled at him once she confirmed her suspicion. Standing back up, she started rinsing the rest of the suds off.

"You know this is just a test, right?" Block informed her.

"What type of test?" she asked, looking puzzled.

"To see how you can work a hose." He smiled wryly.

"Well, if that's the case, I'm holding the wrong one." She dropped the water pressure hose as she walked towards him and grabbed his dick through his jeans.

He looked around to see if anyone saw them, then at his car before he looked back at her. "Let me holla at you in the car real quick."

As soon as he got in the car, he turned the music down. He already knew no one could see them because of his mirror-tinted windows. If they did, they would only be looking at themselves.

She got in and closed the door on the passenger side while he leaned his seat back. She looked at him seductively like she could eat him alive, then said, "Let me show you how I work and drain a hose."

"Umm, I'm loving that," Block moaned.

She started jacking him off and sucking on it at the same time. He looked down to watch her work, seeing some saliva go down the side of his dick. As she did her thing, he put his right hand on the back of her neck.

"Ooh, uhuh. Yeah, you doing that." She made a slurping sound, smacking on his manhood. As she grabbed his balls and licked down to his left sack, she put it in her mouth and started french kissing it softly while jacking him him off at the same time. Then all of a sudden, she grabbed the base of his balls and put both of them both in her mouth.

"Mmmmhmm," she started, humming on his balls.

"Man, what the fuck? You some type of dickologist or something? That shit right there is therapeutic."

"That is the game plan," she mumbled with a mouth full of dick.

"Damn, that feels good." He reached over with his right hand, sticking it in her shorts while she was bent over handling him.

To his surprise, she didn't have any panties on. *That's why that camel toe pussy print was so fat. My type of chick,* he thought, sliding his index and middle finger inside of her. He could feel how wet she was before he even stuck them all the way in her.

"Damn, you so wet," he said as he continued to slide his fingers deeply in her.

"Ummmm." She let out a loud moan, while still sucking.

She started sucking his dick with no hands, just pulling on it with her jaw muscles. He took his hand from out of her shorts and saw how wet and sticky his fingers were. Then looked down at her while she was looking up at him. He couldn't help but lick the juices from off of his fingers

As he smacked on the side of his fingers, he said, "Damn, you taste like a shot of Vodka. You'll get a nigga drunk for real." Then he heard as his cell phone went off.

*Ring, Ring.*

"Damn, who the fuck is this? What the fuck this nigga want now?" Block looked at the screen on his phone. "Hello!"

"What up, fam?" Skalez said.

"I—I'm in the middle of something right now," Block replied, fighting hard not to stutter.

Christy had him way back near her tonsils.

"Man, what the fuck wrong with you?" Skalez asked curiously.

"Don't stop. Keep going," Block instructed her in a low voice, wanting her to continue.

"What you say?" asked Skalez.

"Aye look, ca—call me back a little later." Block hung up.

When he got off the phone, Christy went haywire. She felt his balls tightening and his dick stiffened. She knew he was about to cum, so she slowly took all him in until she gagged a little.

As he grabbed the side of her head with both hands, he released every drop in her mouth. She pulled back slowly and while coming off his dick, her mouth made a popping sound. Then she swallowed his semen slowly, so he can see her throat move as she did it.

"Now, let me ask you a question," Christy said.

"And what's that?" he replied.

"Did I pass the test?"

# Chapter 8

When they were done at the car wash and Christy left, Block decided to call Skalez back.

*Ring, Ring, Ring.*

"Yo, what's good? You done having your moment?" Skalez asked Block, knowing what his boy was doing when he called.

"Yeah, I wish I had that moment for life," Block replied.

"Which one was it?" Skalez asked.

"That snow bunny from Magic City I met the other night."

"Oh yeah?"

"Yeaaah, and she like that, too."

"Like what?"

"Like that. Her mouth felt like some new pussy," said Block, while Skalez started laughing.

"Damn, somebody else calling me," Skalez told him, looking at his cell phone. "Oh, that's 40. Let me link him in." He connected all of them so they could talk. "What's good, 40 ounce?"

"Nigga, now you know why they call me 40. You better act like you know."

"Whatever. But look, I'm glad I got both of y'all on the phone," Skalez said.

"Both of who?" 40 asked curiously.

"Me and you, dumb nigga," Block replied.

"Oh shit, I didn't know you was on here. What's up?"

"Ain't shit. Aye, you remember that snow bunny from the tittie bar the other night?"

"Yeah, the one you was tricking on," 40 replied.

"Nigga, I know you ain't talking. But look, shorty head fire for real. Shorty was pulling on my dick so hard, I thought she was trying to suck my ass hole through my dick head," Block said sarcastically. Skalez and 40 busted out laughing.

"A'ight, a'ight, Hugh Heffener. We can talk about the playboy bunny later," Skalez said, still laughing. "All right, let's get to business. Look, I need both of y'all to meet me at the pier on Chesapeake Bay Avenue," Skalez advised them.

"Where you at now?" 40 asked Skalez.

"I'm at the crib."

"Why we can't come over there?"

"Cause Paula on her bullshit again."

"Yeah, I ain't trying to be around her crazy ass," Block said.

"That's what I'm trying to tell you," Skalez added.

"But why meet at the pier?" 40 asked.

"Cause the water helps me think better and stop asking all them damn questions. Just be there in 45 minutes. It's 5:05 now," Skalez said and hung up, disconnecting all of them.

When the three of them arrived at the little waterfront an hour later, they started walking down the pier.

"So, how we going to go about this with ole' boy?" 40 asked.

"All right, look," Skalez started to say as they reached the end of the pier. "The day we get 'em is going to be the next time him and Tashia are together. But the thing is, we gotta hit both spots at the same time to save time and to not risk anything," Skalez said.

"So how we gon' to do that?" 40 asked, wanting to know.

"See, I was thinking we wait him out at whatever destination they plan to go to. If they get a hotel afterwards, then that's even better. But it really don't matter, either way his ass is going in that trunk," Skalez said.

"How we gonna know which one is which?" Block asked.

"Y'all know how this shit work. He gonna tell us or his ass gonna get tortured," Skalez said with a grim look.

"Now that's what I call foreplay," 40 said.

"We are going to need two cars on standby," Skalez told them.

"I can handle that," 40 assured him.

"Alright, but after we split up and go separate houses, we will contact each other after we our arrive to our destinations. I also have two throw away phones in the car. I had little Tonya go get 'em from Walmart earlier. The only number you dial on these phones is the other burner," Skalez advised them.

"Sounds good, but who's going with who?" Block asked.

"I thought about that also. Y'all know BJ, right?" Skalez asked.

"You talking about Lil BJ from 36 street?" 40 responded quickly.

"Yeah, him!"

"But what about him?"

"He gon' be the driver and look out for you," Skalez said, looking at 40.

"For who?" 40 looked back at Skalez like he was crazy.

"For you."

"Why you pick this young ass nigga?" 40 asked, looking at Skalez like he couldn't believe it. "That little nigga ain't nothing but seventeen years old." 40 was clearly aggravated about the situation.

"And what was your ass doing at seventeen? Nigga you were robbing everyone blind," Skalez reminded him, knowing that would ease his mind some. "Plus, I like the young nigga."

"You only like him cause you used to fuck his sister," 40 said.

"Yeah, you might be right. But I know the little man about his business and he ain't doing nothing but driving and sitting in the car watching out for you any way."

"Yeah, a'ight. You think we will need a mask?" 40 asked.

"Naw, crazy nigga. You only going in the crib and getting the money. It's not like you breaking in. You got the key. Me and Block ain't gonna need no masks neither when we throw ole' boy ass in the trunk. Our faces gon' be the last ones he see anyway."

"So, when all this going to take place?" Block asked.

"Soon as Tashia gives me the word on him. But she gon' let me know ahead of time. So y'all just be on standby and get that car, 40. I'ma let y'all know when it's time to punch the clock. More than likely, it's tomorrow," Skalez said.

"This nigga Lance don't even have an idea about what's about to happen to his ass," 40 said, grinning.

"Oh yeah, another thing," Skalez remembered. "Lil BJ don't know nothing about Lance and the other business that we doing. He only knows about the stash house. He thinks it's just an easy task."

"Oh, I already know! That lil' nigga wasn't about to cut in on my ends. But let's just hope this nigga got some serious cash," 40 said.

"For real, for real! I'm trying to chill out and put up the mask and guns for a while and do something positive with this cash and the rest of this shit I got," Skalez said modestly.

"I feel you on that," Block replied.

"Aye look, I'm 'bout to peel out," Skalez told them, looking at his G-Shock watch for the time. "What y'all doing on this Friday night?"

"Shit, I'm hungry. I'm 'bout to go get something to eat from Pearly's Grill off the avenue," 40 said, rubbing his stomach.

"I'm thinking about meeting back up with Christy," Block said.

"Who the fuck is Christy?" 40 and Skalez asked at the same time.

"The snow bunny," Block replied, smiling.

"Damn, snow flake got you open like that?" Skalez asked, shaking his head. "Shorty must got some good ass head for real!"

"Man, that bitch pussy probably wide as shit. Fucking her probably like throwing a hot dog down a hallway. Ain't gonna feel shit," 40 joked.

"Y'all crazy. A look, I gotta take care of something at home base," Skalez said, walking off.

"Oh yeah? Paula tripping on that ass, huh?" 40 yelled as Skalez was walking back down the pier.

"Yeah, she saying I don't spend enough time with her like I used to and she also got something to holla at me about," Skalez said back and kept walking.

*\*\*\**

"Yes, I will take the All-American Meal with hash browns and extra cheese on the eggs, please," Paula said to the waitress.

"Anything to drink?" the waitress asked.

"Yes, an orange juice, please," Paula replied.

"Not a problem, ma'am. And for you, sir?"

"I'll take a T-bone steak, eggs, cheese grits and a Welch's grape juice to drink," Skalez said to the waitress.

"Why you choose to come to Denny's?" Skalez asked Paula.

"I don't know. I just was craving some breakfast food," she replied.

"You were craving, huh? You said that like you are pregnant or something," Skalez said, smiling.

Paula gave him a serious look, then said, "Because I am pregnant, Jermaine."

His smile faded away, then he asked her if she was serious, but he knew she was when she called him by his first name.

"Serious as the heartbeat that's growing inside of me and why you looking at me like that?"

"Because I was just thinking earlier that I was going to fall back from all the street life and nonsense."

"So, what are you thinking now?" Paula asked, looking into Skalez eyes. Then he started smiling with a huge smile.

"I'm thinking about what life has to offer us and the life growing inside you. Baby, that's the best news I have had since my brother died. How many weeks are you?"

"One month," she said as the waiter approached and gave them their drinks and walked off.

"And you just now telling me?"

"I just found out earlier when I went to the doctor," she answered.

Skalez sighed, then said, "Listen, Paula. We going to do everything together, so don't think you are alone. I'm happy that you are bringing my child into this world." He then reached for her hand across the table. "I can't see me without you."

Paula's eye's started to tear up as Skalez told her how he felt.

"Baby, don't cry," he told her, catching the tear that fell from her eye with his thumb.

"You know we been through a lot together ever since we've known each other and even though I do all this dirt, I still pray to The Most High for us a whole lot—"

"You know I love you so much, Jermaine," Paula interjected, cutting him off.

He felt her love and seriousness when she called him by his government. As they gave each other a light kiss over the table, the waitress brought them their food with a smile.

"At least somebody in this crazy place is happy," the waitress said.

"Yeah, I'm about to be a father," Skalez said, smiling and sitting back down.

"Congratulations!" the waitress replied. "Is there anything else I can get the lovely couple?"

"No, thank you. That's all for now," Paula replied.

\*\*\*

*I'm in love with a stripper*
*She rocking, she rolling, she open*
*She climbing that pole,*
*And I'm in love with a stripper*

T-Pain's song was heard from the speakers in the strip club, Liquid Blue. 40 and Block nodded their head to the music with two strippers in the booth with them in the back of the club.

"Yeah, I'm liking this scenery a little better than Magic City," 40 said.

"Yeah me, too," Block replied, looking at the tall, chocolate stallion bounce her ass in front of him.

"Hey, hey!" 40 said, waiving down one of the waitress that was standing by.

"Yes, would you like something, cutie?" the short small red-boned waitress asked, coming to their booth.

"Yeah, let me get a bottle of Belvedere," 40 said.

"Make that two bottles!" Block yelled.

"I see you two gentlemen want that hard liquor, huh?" the waitress said.

"Yeah, that wine shit make my stomach hurt, but that liquor makes my gun bang hard," Block replied with a smile, while the stripper was still in front of him dancing.

"Oh yeah, which one?" the waitress asked, but didn't wait for a response, walking off to get their bottles. 40 pulled the brown-skinned stripper in front of him onto his lap.

"What you doing tonight after you leave here?" 40 asked the stripper in her ear so he wouldn't have to yell.

"Going with you if you want me to," she replied with the cut cards.

"Damn, I like that. A straightforward bitch. Well look, go get something to write my number down 'cause me and my partner ain't gonna be here all night."

"We talking dollars, right?" the stripper asked, while moving her neck around some.

"Come on, shorty. That's neither here nor there. I'm willing to pay to play. Shit, I'm supporting your hustle right now. Fair exchange ain't never been a robbery," 40 said back.

"Ain't no question. Let me go get that pen and paper real quick," she told him, getting up.

*Money hungry skeezer. Shit, can't blame her,* 40 thought as he watched her ass bounce with every step she took. While he was watched her walking away, the waitress came back with their bottles and two glasses.

"Here y'all go, sweeties," the waitress said. 40 paid for the bottles and handed her a $50 tip.

"Thank you," she replied, smiling before she walked off. The tall stallion that was dancing for Block, walked off right after the waitress left.

"I'ma hit that shit tonight," Block said out loud, looking at the stripper walk away.

"Yeah, well I got that other joint tonight, too," 40 said.

"Oh shit! Look who just walked in the fucking door," Block announced, nodding his hand towards the entrance.

"That nigga don't even know all his money is about to be repoed and a death warrant is out on his head," 40 said.

"Yeah, that nigga better spend some money now and live life to the fullest like it's his last," Block spoke.

"Shit, I hope he don't spend too much," 40 said, looking at Block.

"Man, you crazy. It's the nigga last night on earth! Let'em have some fun. That nigga got a little nice entourage with him, too."

"Fuck that nigga and his entourage. That nigga got a first-class ticket to hell. Shit, I might give him a letter to give to Satan to tell 'em fuck him, too," 40 said, downing a glass of Belvedere Vodka.

"Arghhhh," 40 said, swallowing the liquor. "Damn, that bitch thighs fat," he then said, watching the stripper walk back over to their table.

"So, what's your number?" she asked 40.

40 answered with his digits.

"You never told me your name," she said.

"You can call me U."

"You mean U, like the letter?"

"Yeah, that's it," 40 replied, lying about his name. What's yours?"

"Butterfly," she replied. "Oh yeah, my friend told me in the back that you two are supposed to get together." She turned to Block, waiting for his response.

"Yeah, that's a bet," he acknowledged.

"Well look, we can all get up later and have some fun if y'all for it. Me and Black Chyna can put on a show that's out of this world for y'all," the stripper said, then licked her lips.

"Sounds good to me," 40 said, smiling.

"Cool! I'ma hit you up when we done here," she said, then walked off bouncing her ass and putting on a show for the guys.

"That's what I'm talking about. Aye, you a funny nigga, too," Block said, laughing at the name 40 gave the stripper.

"Shit, she might know somebody that knows somebody. You know how these stripper bitches get around here. We might've killed her brother or something," 40 said being sarcastic, but serious at the same time.

Block and 40 chilled for a while, getting tipsy and watching Lance and he and his crew went threw money. As they watched Lance, someone was watching them at the bar across the room.

They really looking at Block and couldn't believe what they saw when he walked passed them earlier. He threw his last shot of Hennessy back and swallowed hard, then left out the strip club. Ten minutes later, 40 and Block were headed out the door.

"Where you trying to get something to eat from?" 40 asked Block.

"It don't matter to me. I'm with you, you driving," Block replied.

When they walked outside, Block adjusted his gun on his hip. As they were walking to the side of the building to get in 40's truck, some guy was walking towards them with his hat low and a hoodie on.

When Block and 40 saw him reach for his hip like he was getting his cell phone, they both looked at him, but he pulled out a gun and started shooting.

*Bock, Bock, Bock, Bock!*

Block and 40 saw him pulling it off his hip, so they ran behind a Honda Accord and pulled out their guns. The guy then started fast pacing backwards. Block and 40 stood up side by side, then started shooting.

*Bong, Bong, Bong!*

*Pop, Pop, Pop, Pop, Pop!*

The guy started running when he heard the first shot. By the third shot, he fell to the ground, then got back up quickly, limping away real fast before he disappeared around the corner.

"I think I hit that nigga!" Block said, breathing heavily.

"Yo, who the fuck was that?" 40 yelled with anger.

"Fam, I don't know. Let's get the fuck out of here before the police or somebody shows up!" Block yelled.

# Chapter 9

Lil Chris parked down the street after he saw one of guys wearing his dead brother's chain.

"Damn, one of them niggas shot me in the leg," Lil Chris yelled, driving off in his old Acura Legend.

*I gotta get to the hospital before I bleed to death. If police or the people at the hospital, ask me how I got shot and where did it take place at, I'll tell them somebody tried to rob me.*

*Damn, I wish I would've killed off them niggas. I don't even know where these niggas from or where they be at. I should've followed their asses instead of acting on my emotions.*

"Arghhh, damn! This shit burning! You almost there, you almost there," he said, boosting himself up. Then he heard the Clipse's "Grinding" song, which was the ringertone coming from his cell phone.

He picked up and answered. "Yo, who this?"

"What's good, fam?" Lil BJ greeted his partner.

"Man, I just got shot!"

"You what?"

"I said I just got shot! I'm on my way to Riverside Hospital!"

"Oh shit! A'ight, I'm on my way." *Click.*

*＊＊＊*

After reaching the hospital and parking, Lil Chris reached over and grabbed the Burger King bag that was on the passenger seat and placed his gun inside it. Getting out the car and limping to the emergency entrance, he threw the bag in the trashcan out front.

Lil Chris was Peanut's little brother. When Chris found out that his older brother and his crew got robbed and killed, his heart was broken and didn't know which way to turn. His mother was a junkie, so he couldn't turn to her because she was always chasing a high. He lost the only person that mattered to him.

He always looked up to his brother. He was his lifeline, but when he found his body, he knew he would kill whoever he saw wearing his chain. At the age of eighteen and following his big brother's footsteps into the drug trade at a slow pace, he and his right-hand man, Lil BJ, was trying to make a name for themselves, coming up by all means necessary.

*** 

"Yo, somebody just tried to take our motherfucking heads off!" 40 yelled, driving down Jefferson Avenue like a madman.

"That nigga couldn't even aim. But did you get a look at the nigga face?" Block asked.

"All I saw was that nigga gun," 40 said seriously, driving at least 60 miles per hour in a 45 zone.

"Aye yo, you need to slow your roll and take your foot off that gas pedal. You know how these Newport News cops are," Block reminded him, looking at 40. 40 just looked at him, mad as shit, and then he eased his foot off the gas some.

"I don't know why you looking at me like that!" As soon as Block said that, 40's cell phone started ringing.

"Who dis?" 40 answered loudly when he picked up.

"Damn, fam! If I didn't know who you were, I would've been scared as shit the way you answered the phone," Skalez said joking, not knowing it wasn't a time to be playing games.

"Some bullshit just happened with me and Block."

"Like what?"

"Some nigga just shot at us at Liquid Blue, trying to take out a nigga."

"For real!" Skalez clenched his teeth together. "Did you see who it was?" Skalez asked.

"Naw."

"Y'all wanna meet up real quick?"

"For what? You can't do nothing about it. But guess who we saw in the strip joint?"

"Who?"

"Your boy, Lance. He rolled in with his mini entourage, just throwing money around and shit."

"Yeah? He better enjoy every last dollar he spent."

"Aye yo, look. Let me get off this phone real quick. You know how the police are around this bitch."

"A'ight. Hit me up in the morning and you two niggas stay out the way."

"Shit, it's like the more I try to stay out the way, the more I'm in the way. A'ight, I'm gone, fam," 40 said, disconnecting the call.

"Man, this shit crazy for real!" Block said when 40 hung up.

"I knew I should've got up with my snow bunny tonight."

"Yeah, well you didn't."

"Aye, yo, take me to get my car."

"Why? What you about to do?"

"Shit, I'ma call it a night," Block said.

"So, you ain't trying to get up with them hoes from the strip club?"

"Nigga, is you crazy? My dick probably won't even get up. Take me to get my shit." Block looked at him like he was crazy.

"Well shit! I'ma call it a night also," 40 replied.

***

"I got here as quick as I could, but the nurse said I couldn't come back there," Lil BJ told him.

"Yeah? They was taking the bullet out my leg. They said I lost a lot of blood," Lil Chris explained.

"You need me to call your mom?"

"Hell naw! She probably out looking for a hit right now," Lil Chris said, looking angry because he knew the only person he had like family was Lil BJ.

"A'ight, but what happened? And where did this take place at?"

Before Lil Chris responded, he looked at Lil BJ for a second, then he started looking at the ground.

"I think I saw the niggas that robbed and killed my brother," Lil Chris said in a low voice.

"Oh yeah? You know who they are or where they be at?"

"Naw, I fucked that up! Now I probably ain't gone never catch them niggas!"

"Where the fuck was you and how you know it was them niggas who killed your brother?" Lil BJ asked anxiously, but was curious at the same time.

"You know the strip club, Liquid Blue, right?"

"Yeah."

"Well, I went there for a couple drinks and to look at some of the girls. While I was walking to the bar, I saw two dudes pass me. You know my brother's chain is one of a kind. He just got it made three weeks before he died."

"Yeah, I remember when he hopped out the LS 400 with that big ass chain swinging from his neck, smiling hard as shit with them golds in his mouth," Lil BJ replied, thinking back.

"Yeah," Lil Chris said lowly, staring at the wall. "But check it, as I was walking towards them, I saw one of the guy's chain shining hard from the blue light and it caught my attention. So, when I got close enough to look at it, I saw them two red rubies he had in the eyes of the Jesus piece."

"So, what happened after that? You know, that led to you getting shot."

"Man, just listen! After I saw that shit, I went straight to the back and got a couple of drinks. You know them niggas don't I.D. nobody, but I watched them for a while. But the more I saw my brother's chain around his neck, the angrier I became. So, I walked out the club and waited for them to come out. I parked my car around the corner, then I walked back towards the club. As I was coming from the back, I saw them coming from around the side of the building headed in my direction. I couldn't set up like I wanted to, so I upped my Glock and started shooting."

"Did you get 'em?"

"It's like them niggas knew I was coming for their ass or something, 'cause soon as I got close to them, them niggas ran on the side of a car for cover. Then they opened fire on me when I started running away."

"Both of 'em started shooting?"

"Hell yeah! It sounded like I was over Iraq or some shit."

"Nigga, you lucky your ass still breathing. Why the fuck you ain't call me first before you made a move?"

"Man, I don't know!" Lil Chris told him, shaking his head. "I just wanted to get my brother's chain back and who did him in."

"Did you at least see what they were driving?"

"Nope!"

"Shit! It's just a lose lose situation. How long they say you gotta stay up in this hospital?"

"Just until tomorrow. But shit, I'm cool for real! They already patched me up and shit. As a matter of fact, I'm up outta this bitch," Lil Chris said, hopping off the bed looking for his pants, then he remembered he told the nurse to throw them away because of all the blood on them.

"You sure?" You ain't got nothing but your shirt and boxers on," Lil BJ said, looking at Lil Chris like he was crazy hopping around.

"Yeah, I'm cool. They got the bullet out already and I got another pair of pants in my car," Lil Chris replied, grabbing the crutches on the wall before he limped out the door.

He walked down the hallway with just his shirt, boxers, and shoes on with Lil BJ on the side. The hospital was busy on a Saturday at 3:45 in the morning. As they walked, no one asked Lil Chris any questions. They exited out the entrance they came in. Then Lil Chris looked around and noticed no one was around before he started digging through the trashcan.

"Aye yo, what the fuck is you doing?" Lil BJ asked, looking at him like he was crazy. Lil Chris didn't respond until he found what he was looking for.

"Here it go," he said, getting up and grabbing his crutches. "Here, take this," Lil Chris said, passing the Burger King bag to BJ.

"Damn, homie. If you were hungry, we could've stop somewhere and got you something to eat. This shit kinda heavy," Lil BJ said as they were walking to Lil Chris' car. He opened the bag. "Oh yeah! That's a big whopper. What the fuck you put it in the trash can for?" Lil BJ then closed the bag.

"Because if the police would've came and questioned me or took a look in my car at least, I would've been clean, you feel me?"

"No doubt," Lil BJ replied.

"How you get up here anyway?"

"I drove my shorty's car. You wanna come back later and get your car because your leg all fucked up?"

"Hell naw! Shit, it only takes one leg to drive anyway," Lil Chris said, getting in the car.

"A'ight, super thug," Lil BJ shot back with a smirk.

"What you 'bout to do?"

"I'm 'bout to head to my shorty's crib! What you 'bout to do?"

"I'ma head to the crib and pop some Motrin or some type of pain medicine. I know my pipe-headed momma got something in there to ease the pain."

"Come back, fam. We only get one momma, so value her. Just hope she breaks the habit."

"Yeah whatever! It's not gonna happen. The only thing she gonna break is her legs try'na run to get a hit."

"Man, you wild. But look, I'ma holla at you tomorrow. I got something plan and if it turns out good, we gonna be alright!"

"What kind business you got plan for tomorrow?"

"Don't worry 'bout all that. Just know I got you. I'ma holla at you later," Lil BJ said, dapping him up before they parted ways.

# Chapter 10

As morning came rolling around, Skalez rubbed his eyelids, then looked around and got out of bed. *Damn, something smells good,* he thought, headed to where the aroma was coming from. As he was walking down the stairs, he heard Robin Thicke's "Lost Without You" coming from the radio in the living room. Walking into the kitchen, Paula said, "Good morning, sleepy head."

"Good morning to you too, baby. You got it smelling all good in here," Skalez replied.

"Yup, just for your stinky breath."

"Ahhhhh," Skalez said, blowing his morning breath near her face.

"Come on, stop. That's not funny."

"Come on and give daddy a kiss." Skalez poked out his lips.

"Stop playing and go sit down while I finish cooking." She pushed him away from the stove area.

"Alright, I'll be quiet and go sit down. But after we eat, I'll be talking again."

"Boy, you so silly," Paula said, while stirring the eggs in the pan.

"You know what I was thinking?" Skalez asked, sitting down at the dining room table.

"No, what?"

"Before the baby is born, I think we should move into a bigger house, somewhere uptown or something. What you think?"

"For real?" Paula felt ecstatic.

"Yeah, we are going to need the space. The townhouse is cool and all, but it's 'bout time we upgrade."

"So, when are we going to go look at some properties?" Paula asked excitedly.

"Real soon! I gotta handle something first because when we go, I wanna make sure the house we really like is the one we get right then."

"Baby, I love you so much!" Paula gushed, placing his plate of breakfast in front of him and giving him a kiss.

"Oh! Now you wanna kiss me, huh?"

"Stop it, baby. It's not like that! You know I'm just glad that you're going to leave those streets alone. You know I couldn't stand to see something happen to you," she said, standing as she looked at him.

"When you told me you were pregnant, that really stamped it for me to cool off. Baby, you in good hands like Allstate. I'ma be there for you both, believe that. I just gotta handle one more situation."

After they ate and discussed future plans, Skalez took a shower, got dressed and left. While riding down Wariack Boulevard, his phone started to ring. He looked at it and immediately answered it.

"Tell me something good."

"Depends on what you wanna hear," Tashia replied.

"Anything pertaining to money."

"Well in that case, the money man is looking good right about now. Where you at, pretty boy?"

"I'm in traffic. Why, what's up?"

"I need you to come through so I can holla at you about that."

"All right, I'm on my way now."

"Hey, before you come here, stop by KFC and get me some honey BBQ wings."

"Damn, do I look like a delivery boy to you?"

"No, but you look like the guy that took my virginity and popped my cherry," Tashia said with emphasis.

"Why you always bringing that shit up for? Like you gonna get a prize or something."

"Why I can't? You damn sure got my prize."

"Shorty, you crazy as shit. I gotcha. I'll see you in ten."
Skalez hung up. *I know she still has feelings for a nigga but that chapter in life is done*, Skalez thought. While riding to the fast food restaurant, he was lost in his thoughts.

\*\*\*

"Welcome to KFC. May I take your order?" the voice said, coming from the menu speaker as he pulled up to the KFC.

"Uh, yeah. Let me get the honey BBQ meal."

"And what would you like to drink?"

"Coke with light ice," he replied, knowing how much Tashia complained about how much ice they put in your drink to shorten your beverage.

"Six dollars and six-five cents at the first window," he heard. As he reached the first window, he handed the cashier a ten-dollar bill and drove off to the second window. He sat for a minute, then the window opened.

"Excuse me, sir. You forgot to get your change," the cashier said, staring at Skalez.

"I know, but it's cool. Keep it."

"I can't take your money. It's against the policy," she replied, passing him his food. Then she said before turning around, "Hold on."

She came back a couple seconds later and handed him his change with a smile. He realized that she was easy on the eyes and really pretty.

As he took the money, she said, "I hope you use it."

"Use what?" he asked, wanting to know what she was referring to.

"Your money."

As he looked down in his hand, he saw red ink on one of the dollar bills and realized it was her number.

"I might just do that," he said back with a smile.

"I hope so," she replied, grinning.

Skalez was always a sucka for a pretty smile. He looked at her for a couple of seconds and said, "A'ight." Then he pulled off.

"I still got it, but shit, I ain't never lose it," he said out loud to himself. He looked at the dollar bill with her number, then threw it out the sunroof of his Beamer. "I won't be needing that."

Reaching downtown at Tashia's apartment, he called her before actually pulling up, telling her to unlock the door. Knowing her, she probably had the music blasting and would have him banging on her door for a half hour.

Skalez hopped out his 750 series BMW with her KFC meal and started walking towards her door. She opened the door with a bright smile on her face, showing off her deep dimples in her cheeks.

Skalez smiled to himself and nonchalantly said, "What's good?" before he walked pass her. Sitting the food down on the living room table, then flopped back on the sofa sitting down, then asked, "Where the kids at?"

"With their Aunt Tammy for the weekend! I'm glad 'cause I need a break," she told him, closing the door.

"Oh yeah, I bet. But how your sister been doing lately?"

"She's cool. Just got out that crazy relationship with Keith," Tashia replied, while opening the box of chicken. "You want some?" she asked, offering Skalez some of her food, while sitting next to him.

"Naw, I'm good. I'm still full off that big breakfast Paula cooked for me this morning."

"Tsk!" Tashia balled her face up.

"What you looking like that for?"

As soon as he said that, Tashia stared at him for a moment and said, "Listen, Jermaine. You know I still got feelings for you. I mean you were my first. My first everything, my first boyfriend, my first kiss, first love—"

"Listen, Tashia! I got feelings for you also, but it's a different type of feeling. We are grown now. You have a life with two kids and I'm about to have a child myself."

"So, Paula is pregnant?" There was obvious hurt in her voice.

"Yes, I'm about to be a father and I want to be there for my family. Tashia, you will always be family to me and I will always have endless love for you, but—"

"Yeah, whatever, nigga!" Skalez could tell she was *big* mad. "You shouldn't have played me like you did back then and we might've made it out okay. You fucked me up, Jermaine. It's like that Jay-Z's song called "Song Cry". Once a good girl is gone bad, she's gone forever. Nigga, you fucked me up mentally for life. You the reason why I act the way I do towards niggas now, but it will never even out because he ain't you."

"You can't blame me for your faults. Come on, baby girl," Skalez said, opening his arms out, while talking and shaking his head. "And back then, I was young, dumb and full of cum. I'ma man now, so I do what men do. So, it's my responsibility to be a man and take care of mines."

"Then why you can't do that with me?" Tashia asked softly, wishing things were different.

Skalez sighed, and then he slowly explained, "Because Tash, we got two different lives and I'm not about to be stuck in the past."

"Cool. I don't even want to discuss it anymore."

After she let it go, they conversed about how they going to get Lance, then Skalez left.

\*\*\*

While riding down the street, Skalez got caught up in his thoughts, thinking about the should've, could've and what if's.

Tashia used to be a good girl back in the day, always staying out of trouble, going to school without missing a day, and making good grades until she got involved with him.

*I shouldn't have shown her the street life at an early age because sometimes when a person sees that side, they don't make it back. I know she remember vividly what I did to her and everything we did in the streets. It took a while for her to get over me having sex with her friend. I guess you can change a person's outlook on something and fuck it up for the next one because she damn sure is sour now,* he thought to himself.

Looking at the time on his watch, he picked up his cell-phone and started dialing.

"Yo, what's good? Where you at?" Skalez asked after 40 picked up the phone.

"I'm at the crib. Why, what's up?" 40 replied.

"Good! I'm on my way over there. I'll be there in 15 minutes," Skalez said and hung up, then started dialing another number.

"Talk to me, I'll talk back," Block said, answering the phone.

"Well, if both of us talking, one of us ain't listening."

"Well then, I'm all ears," Block shot back.

"I need you to meet me at 40's crib. Where you at?"

"I'm near there."

"A'ight, meet me over there. We gotta discuss some business."

"A'ight, I'm gone," Block replied and disconnected the call.

*** 

Pulling up in front of 40's spot, Skalez beeped his car horn to let him know he was out front. As Skalez was opening his car door, he saw Block's Lexus pulling in. *Good timing,* Skalez thought.

40 opened his front door and came out wearing some Polo sweats, Mike flip flops and a wife beater on with a Corona in his hand.

"What's up, family?" 40 said, smiling.

"Ain't shit. Try'na keep up with this money," Skalez replied.

"What's good with you, you funny looking niggas?" Block said, getting out his car.

"Funny looking! Nigga, you high yellow, albino, German Shepard looking ass nigga. I'm the flyest nigga you ever been around," Skalez boasted, looking at Block up and down. "Man, let's go inside and talk about this money, funny looking ass nigga."

"Damn nigga, you need to learn how to clean up." Block looked around. "You got pizza boxes and beer bottles all through this bitch."

"A typical bachelor crib," 40 said, downing the rest of his beer, while shutting the door after they all went in.

"Bullshit! I'ma bachelor and my shit don't look nothing like this," Block replied quickly.

"That's because you don't party hard like I do. Nigga, I'ma rock star," 40 said, placing the bottle on the table with the rest of the beer bottles.

"A'ight, look," Skalez said, cleaning a spot on the couch for him to sit down.

"This what we gon' do. Lance and Tashia are supposed to go out on the Spirit of Norfolk, the little cruise for a couple of hours."

"Oh, nigga on some romantic shit, huh? Taking her out on the ocean and shit," 40 said, sitting in his Lazy-Boy recliner,

"Yeah, but look, they got reservations at Smitty's for dinner. But they not even gon' make it there for the food! When they go on that little two-hour cruise, they will have to park their car in the parking garage."

"Yeah, I already know where you're headed with this," Block said, sitting on the couch next to Skalez.

"A'ight, but look, depending on how the scenery looks in there, will determine if that's where we make our move. I got all the supplies we need," Skalez relayed. "Oh yeah, and another thing. Tashia's going with you and Lil BJ to the house to make sure y'all find the right house. We don't need no fuck ups and we damn sure don't need her around us at the house when we off this nigga. You," Skalez said, pointing to 40, "and Lil BJ gon' be around the corner on Lake Shore Drive by the dock. That's where we'll meet up to give you the keys to the stash house."

"What happens if the nigga gives us the wrong keys," 40 asked.

"Damn, nigga, you drunk or something 'cause I swear you asked the same damn question when we talked about this before? But it's cool 'cause we just going back over everything. But naw, he ain't gon' do that, believe me," Skalez said with a grim look.

"So, when are we taking our positions 'cause the more we talk about it, my palms get to itching." 40 rubbed his hands together.

"Tonight at 7:00 p.m. The boat ride takes off at 7:30 p.m., so you know he gonna pick her up early. Me and Block will follow them from Tashia's crib, but you and Lil BJ gonna be at the docks already waiting at 6:45 or 7:00. If it's clear in the garage, he won't even make it to the boat. If not, we wait un til they get back. I already got a dark-tinted van. 40, we need you to get that raggedy ass fiend's whip or something."

"Man, that shit might break down on our ass," 40 said. "I'ma try to get something else first, but that will be our last resort."

"Ay, look!" Skalez looked down at his watch. "It's 1:30 p.m. now. We got 6 and a half hours until we make our move and take our places. The clock is ticking. So, with time moving, that means the money moving and we need to be moving with the money.

"Here," Skalez stood up, pulling a piece of paper out his pocket, giving it to 40. "That's Lil BJ's number. Go get 'em as soon as you get the car. Me and Block gonna meet y'all at the pier on Chesapeake Bay Avenue at 6:00 tonight, so do what y'all gotta do before then. Block, I'ma pick you up at 5:30," Skalez told them, opening the door to leave.

"No fuck ups, ladies. Time to punch the clock," Skalez said, shutting the door before they could say anything.

# Chapter 11

Later on, a few hours later, they all met up as planned. Even Lil BJ was there ready to put in some work. "What's good, lil' homie?" Skalez said, dapping up Lil BJ.

"Ain't nothing. Ready to get this paper," Lil BJ replied.

"I know that's right. All you gotta do is hold down 40 while he go up in the crib and retrieve the case. Just sit in the car and make sure nothing looks suspicious." Lil BJ just nodded his head at every word he spoke. "It's as easy as taking candy from a baby."

"How much you think gon' be in the crib?"

"It should be a good amount."

"Where you and Block gonna be at?"

"Nowhere around there. Too many people know us around there. Plus, we will be tailing him for a brief moment, then bring y'all the keys," Skalez said agitated, playing him to the left.

"How much I'ma get off the break down?" Lil BJ asked.

40, Block and Skalez looked at him like he was crazy.

"Damn, you asking a lot of questions for a person that isn't doing much," Skalez told him firmly. "But check this out, everybody don't get paid the same. It's like being on a NBA team. The center is not going to get the same pay as the point guard. Everybody got a position to play and everyone's position doesn't require the same work. You on the bench right now! You're the driver. You're just watching the game play out right now. If we need some assistance, that's when you come into play. As a matter of fact, I don't even know why I am explaining this to you," Skalez spoke with bass in his voice. "I just brought you along on this little easy money scheme because I fuck with you and I thought your little ass could use the money."

"Naw, my nigga, I got it! I'ma play my position," Lil BJ replied, but he really was angry about how he went off on him in front of his boys.

"A'ight, let's break," Skalez told them as he walked off, heading towards the van with Block on his side.

*** 

"Hey, baby," Tashia said, getting in the car and giving Lance a kiss.

"You looking good, as usual," he complimented her, adding a smile.

"Thank you! You don't look too bad yourself."

"Yeah, you bring out the best in me," Lance remarked, putting the car in gear and driving off.

"You know I've never been on the Spirit of Norfolk before," Tashia said, looking over at Lance.

"Well, that's good. Now we can share our first at something together because I haven't either."

As they reached their destination and parked in the parking garage, he looked around and saw a few people.

"Well, I guess that's a good thing," Lance said.

"And what's that?" Tashia asked.

"That it's not crowded down here tonight."

Stepping out the car, the little breeze blew Tashia's black, knee-high Gucci dress a little. Feeling the breeze through her legs, gave her pussy a chill because she wasn't wearing any panties. As they continued to walk, Lance didn't realize he had two sets of eyes watching him.

"Damn, Tashia looking good in that black dress and heels," Block said, watching her walk off with Lance.

"Yeah, she looks cool," Skalez said nonchalantly.

"I remember when you used to fuck with shorty back in the day. Fam, you fucked that girl head up, for real!" Block said with a smirk, shaking his head.

"Why you say that?"

"Look at her. That's not her. I mean, it's her now, but shorty used to be on some straight goodie-two-shoe shit. Since you fucked her over, she been looking for love in all the wrong places and money ain't one of them."

"Yeah, you might be right."

"Nigga, I know I'm right. After y'all broke up, she went dick and money crazy. She had her first baby at 16 years old, then followed by another a year later. She been going downhill ever since. She still looks good as shit, though," Block said, while watching her walk off.

"Man, fuck all that. Time changes and when time changes, people change and right now it's time to get this paper," Skalez said, dialing 40 on the burner phone.

"Talk to me," 40 answered on the first ring.

"What's good? Y'all on post?"

"Yeah, we here."

"Well look, they on their way to go on the little cruise, so we'll wait until they come back."

"All right."

"What that little nigga doing?" Skalez asked, referring to Lil BJ.

"He cooling. Just talking a nigga head off."

"Oh yeah?" Skalez heard Lil BJ say in the background.

"Look out for my call in a little bit, a'ight?" Skalez said and hung up, not waiting for a response.

"What Skalez talking about?" Lil BJ asked.

"Nothing. He just said dude still at the crib and he gon' call us when we leave to bring us the key," 40 said, lying to him.

"Oh, a'ight! But like I was saying, while I was banging my shorty back out, my man called me and said he just got shot."

"Oh word?" 40 said, looking at Lil BJ. Before Lil BJ got another word out, 40's cell phone started ringing.

"Talk to me," 40 said into his phone.

"Hey baby! I been missing you," the girl on the other end of the phone said.

"Oh yeah? How much?"

"Too much to explain over this phone. I can show it way better than I can speak it."

"I know that's right." 40 gripped his crotch.

"When I'ma see you again?"

"It might be tonight if the time is right," he said, while getting something out of his pocket. "Here roll this." He passed Lil BJ some weed and a Dutch.

"What you say?" the girl on the phone asked.

"Oh naw, I was talking to my little partner. But yeah, we might get up tonight."

"I hope so because I want to feel you inside of me."

"What you got on right now?"

"Your favorite color," she said in a low sexy tone.

"And what's that?"

"My skin."

"Just make sure you keep that on when I see you."

"You know I got you, baby."

"I know that's right! Ah look, let me get off this phone real quick. I'ma hit you up when I'm done handling this business," 40 said after they talked for a few more minutes.

"Ok, baby. I'll see you later," the female said and blew a kiss through the phone and hung up.

"Let me finish telling you my story," Lil BJ said before he was sent off by 40.

"Nigga, ain't nobody try'na hear that bullshit. You can't even roll a blunt right," 40 said, grabbing the limp blunt.

"Yeah, whatever, nigga. Who was that? One of your shorties?" Lil BJ asked.

"Yeah, straight freak bitch. She'll suck your dick so long until that shit look like a fifty-year-old prune."

"Fam, you wild as shit." Lil BJ laughed.

They stayed in the car and smoked and talked for a while, waiting on Skalez. 40 was on his cell phone for most of the time.

As Lance and Tashia sailed out into the ocean looking out at the moonshine off the ocean water, they both were lost in thought.

"What you thinking about?" Tashia said, breaking the silence.

Lance looked and stared at her for a second, then grabbed the rail of the boat before he responded. "Life. I'm thinking about life."

"What about life?"

"Just the ins and outs. It's like I got everything I need and then I don't. Like I just feel incomplete at times."

Lance took in a deep breath, inhaling the night air into his lungs while looking out over the ocean waters.

"And why's that?" Tashia asked, looking directly at him.

Lance looked at her, then turned his whole body towards hers and replied, "I just feel lonely at times, like I have no one to share my life with. But since we've been hanging out with each other, I've been feeling whole, and that's rare. Truth be told, it's hard to find a woman I can call my own. The money, the clothes, the cars come easy, but it's not the same if you can't share it with someone special." As he grabbed her hand he said, "I'm glad I found you."

Then he leaned in to kiss her. She kissed him and thought that was one of the weakest lines she'd heard in a long time and thought she might have heard it in a movie before.

As they continued to kiss, he grabbed her ass while she let out a small light sigh. He started planting kisses on her neck.

"Not here Lance," Tashia said in a low soft voice, lifting her head back some, enjoying the kisses and his tongue on her neck. He looked around, realizing there was no one on the deck, so he went up her dress from the front, feeling her bare pussy.

After finding out she didn't have any panties on, his dick got rock hard immediately. He started fingering her with just his index finger until her juices started flowing down his fingers. He pulled his hand from underneath her dress and licked them.

"Mmmm, I like the way that taste."

He turned her around and pulled his dick out of the zipper slot while she grabbed on to the rail, looking at the ocean. He lifted her Gucci dress and entered her.

"Ummm, damn you so wet, Tashia," he whispered, biting down on his bottom lip.

"Oh, hit it harder, daddy." Tashia threw her fat ass back on him. She knew he wasn't working with much, but just the thought of them getting caught turned her on.

Grabbing her left shoulder with his left hand and then her waist with his right hand, he started pulling her back, pumping harder and faster.

"Like that, huh?" He watched his dick go in and out of her pussy from the back.

"Yes, Lance! Just like that! Ahhh, ummm," she moaned, while she tucking her lips inside her mouth trying not to be loud. Just looking at her ass jiggle as he was pounding her, enhanced it for him.

"I—I'm about to cum," he growled.

She pushed him off, knelt down and took all of him in her mouth, sucking it until he released all of his cum. His whole body tensed up, then his dick jumped one last time while she pulled in it and squeezed her jaws tightly around it.

Pulling his dick out slowly, she looked up at him and thought, *This nigga better enjoy this because it's gonna be his last shot of pussy for life.* Standing up, she quickly straightened herself up. Then he said, "I never felt this before."

"Felt what?" she asked.

"It's like my whole body went into convulsions."

"I'm glad you enjoyed it because I damn sure did."

"I'm glad I found you, Tashia, for real," he said once again.

Tashia smiled. "Believe me, I'm glad I found you, too."

\*\*\*

After their quick fuck session, they went inside the ship and had a couple of drinks, talking for the rest of the cruise. As they got off the boat and headed to the car garage, Tashia saw there were a few couples headed in the same direction, so she stalled him for five minutes, stopping and talking. Then they continued to walk into the car garage.

As soon as they reached his Benz, he heard the sound of a cocking gun. After turning around, he saw an automatic rifle pointed right at his head. Tashia let out a small scream.

"Shut the fuck up. If I see you move, I'ma leave your head where your feet are standing now," the guy with the gun said.

Then a van came to a fast halt and another guy jumped out.

"You can take everything I got." Lance put his hands in the air, thinking they just wanted the case in his pockets.

"Oh, we gon' get everything you got, believe that," the guy with the gun said. "Put the cuffs on this nigga."

After the other guy handcuffed him, the guy with the gun hit 'em with the handle of the gun and knocked Lance clean out. After they put him in the van, the guy with the gun went in his pockets and got his keys.

The other guy got on the driver's side and drove off slowly with Tashia in the passenger seat.

"Wake up!" the guy in the back said to Lance, smacking him violently.

"Go the speed limit," the guy in the back seat told the driver.

Pulling out the taser, the guy hit Lance with some volts to his ribs. Lance shook like he had the Holy Ghost.

"Oh, you awake now, huh? I'ma ask you one time. Which one of these keys is the one to your stash house?"

Lance looked at the man scared as hell, wondering how did he know about his stash crib. *Damn, I got caught slipping,* Lance thought.

"I don't—" was all he got out before he felt more voltage going through his neck from the taser, his head jumping back and forth uncontrollably.

"Ok, ok!" Lance pleaded, shaking like a 1957 Chevy. "The one next to my car key. The one with the gold trimming around the top."

"Now, that wasn't hard, was it?" Skalez mocked him. "If you lie to me again, I'm a put this taser to your nuts," the guy said.

"I swear that's it!" Lance shivered.

"Listen, I'm not going to kill you. I just need your cooperation, a'ight," the guy said, then reached in the bag next to him and pulled out some duct tape and a pillow case. He ripped off a piece of tape, then put it around his mouth. Next, he put the pillowcase over Lance's head.

"Mmm, mmm," Lance mumbled.

As they reached a dock on Lakeshore Drive, the guy that was in the back got out of the van with Tashia behind him. They went over to another car where two more guys were.

"When you get into the house, call me immediately," one of the guys said, handing over a key.

"Tashia, make sure they find the right house. Handle y'all business," he said and ran back to the van and hopped in.

"Time to go for a little ride!"

# Chapter 12

*I never thought it would end like this,* Lance thought as he lay across the back seat of the van cuffed with a pillowcase over his head. A lot was going through his head. He had a son he barely saw in New York and a mother that was still fighting cancer.

*Damn, this nigga didn't even have a mask on. They gonna to kill me,* he thought getting more scared and nervous by the second. He didn't even remember what happened to Tashia after he got hit with the gun.

*I hope she all right. Shit, I hope I be all right,* he thought. As soon as they reached Lance's house, Skalez's burner phone rung.

"What's good on that end?" Skalez asked.

"Aye look, I'm in the crib, but I don't see no stash. No safe or nothing," 40 said back into his phone. "I cut up the couch, the mattress in both rooms and took the T.V. apart. I even went up in his dusty ass attic."

"All right, sit tight for one second. We at this nigga's crib now," Skalez replied and hung up.

As him and Block got out, the sensor light came on and startled him for a quick second. They grabbed Lance out of the van, ripped the duct tape from around the pillowcase, and pulled both of them off. Lance's vision was blurry at first, but when he looked around and realized where they were, his eyes got big as two silver dollars.

"Mmmmm. Mmmmm," he moaned as he started to panic with the tape still around his mouth and hands cuffed.

"I know you're wondering what we're doing here. You should already know by now." Skalez held Lance up from falling.

"You got a nice piece of property right here, Lance. Neighbors live a quarter mile away from each other, huh?"

Block said as they were walking up the stairs to the front door. "A lot of land, too."

"Yeah, you were doing it, too," Skalez said, using past tense.

"You got an alarm or any surprises through these doors before we go in?" Block asked, pointing his p89 Ruger at his forehead. "No dogs or nothing, huh?"

Lance just started shaking his head, moaning, "Mmmm. Mmmm."

"Oh, so you ain't scared of people like us breaking in your shit, huh?" Skalez taunted him as he tried a couple keys to open the door before he finally opened the 18-foot double doors.

As they walked in and shut the door, Skalez and Block looked around, taking in their surroundings.

"Damn, playboy. You got marble floors, chandeliers and the whole nine." Block admired Lance's mini mansion.

As they reached a big room down the hallway guessing it was the living room, Skalez pushed him on the sofa. With Lance still being handcuffed, he lost his balance and fell over.

Skalez went over and ripped the tape off his mouth. "Alright listen, bitch ass nigga. All we wanna know is where the money at and we'll leave."

"I know you gonna kill me," Lance said, shaking but hoping they wouldn't.

"If you keep prolonging this, I will! Here, call the other phone," Skalez said, passing the phone to Block.

As Block was dialing the number, he was looked around the huge room they were in and thought, *Damn I need to be living like this* until he heard 40 pick up the phone.

"Damn, a few minutes felt like two hours. Fam, I didn't find nothing but five new pairs of Jordans," 40 said loudly on the speakerphone.

"Hold on, 40." Skalez spoke loud enough to be heard over the speakerphone as Block held it nearby. "A'ight, Lance. Where the money at over the stash house?" Skalez asked as he held the mini-lightening bolt.

"Come on, man. That's all I got to my name. Don't do this to me," Lance pleaded.

"Wrong answer!" Skalez zapped him with the taser.

"Ahhhhhh!" Lance screamed.

"Man, what the fuck!" 40 yelled through the phone, wondering what the hell Skalez was doing to Lance.

"A'ight, a'ight! It's in the room straight in the back under the bed," Lance told him after Skalez stopped tasing him.

"You heard that?" Skalez said.

"Yeah, yeah," 40 replied.

\*\*\*

When 40 reached the back room, he looked at the mattress already ripped up with the knife, then flipped it over and stood it up next to the wall.

"Hey 40, where you at?" Tashia called out, entering the house.

"I'm in the back. What the fuck you doing here?"

"You were taking too long and I wanted to make sure you were alright," she said, walking in the bedroom.

"What's this supposed to be? Some type of joke?" 40 said, picking the phone back up after flipping the mattress over. "It ain't shit up under the bed."

"Oh yeah, mu'fucker. You wanna keep playing games, huh?" Skalez said to Lance.

40 pressed the speaker button on the phone, then handed it to Tashia. Then he knelt down in between the bed brackets.

"Hold on, Skalez," 40 said loud enough to be heard through the phone. "I think I got something." He looked at the cut seam in the carpet. While pulling the carpet back at the seam, a smile crept across his face. "Jackpot!"

"You got it?" Skalez asked.

"Hell yeah. What's the combination?"

"What's the combo, playboy?" Skalez asked Lance.

40 was all ears. He heard Lance call out the numbers.

"You got it?" Skalez asked full of hype.

"You damn right," 40 said excitedly.

"Alright, give Lil BJ five stacks and drop him off. You and Tashia wait on us at the hotel."

"Shit, I damn near got that in my pockets to give 'em "

"Hey, Skalez," Tashia said quickly, holding the phone before Skalez hung up.

"Yeah, what's good? Make it fast."

"Let me speak to my dead boyfriend."

"He already listening," Skalez said, smiling.

When Lance heard Tashia's voice come through the phone, he got sick to his stomach. He couldn't believe what he was hearing. His eyes got wide and his mouth dropped.

"You dirty bitch! You been setting me up the whole time." Lance was mad as shit. He wished he could get his hands around her throat.

"I'll be that, but no hard feelings, baby. It was just business. You are a nice guy and all and I hope you do find that one person you can spend the rest of your life with in another life," Tashia said coldly.

"I'ma kill your ass when I see you!"

"Nigga, you already dead. Catch me in hell, motherfucker. And you better have on your fire boots. I still might be burning your money up when I get there, you little dick bastard." Tashia laughed loudly before she hung up.

Lance thought about his money being taken, and that no good bitch Tashia. Then he thought about the twenty bricks he still had in the deep freezer. They didn't mention that. All they wanted was the money he thought because they didn't ask for any drugs.

*They might let me live. I'll give them money out my little safe upstairs in my office and hopefully they let me walk,* he thought to himself.

"Look, Lance, we don't want to kill you," Block said. "All we want is the money. We know you a hustler, but we don't want the drugs. We gonna let you keep them so you can get back on your feet. Just lead us to the money in here." He said it, making it sound all good. Lance looked at him like he knew just what he was thinking.

"It's upstairs in my office," Lance said dryly.

"A'ight, come on and show us where that is." Skalez helped him get up off the floor.

As they walked up the swirled stairs behind Lance, Skalez was nudging the 45 Desert Eagle in his back.

"Don't try no stupid shit," he warned.

"Come on, son. I ain't tryna die," Lance replied.

When they reached the room on the second floor of the house, they went in his office. They noticed five T.V. monitors on the wall. As they got closer, they themselves on the T.V. screen. Block smacked him in the head with his gun.

"Where the fuck are the tapes to this shit?" Block yelled.

"Arghhh!" Lance screamed from the hit to the head. "It's on the wall next to the screens. Just eject it."

Block hit him.

*I swear I'ma kill these niggas and that bitch too if I make it out of here,* he thought. He'd been in the game too long to know that if a robbery took place like this and they had no masks on, it was probably going to be a homicide. But he was hoping his situation was different.

Skalez got up, went over to the oil painting, threw it off the wall and saw the safe.

"What's the numbers?"

"8, 9, 15," Lance said, looking up at the gun Block had pointed at him. When the safe opened, Skalez began to smile. Then it disappeared quickly.

"What the fuck is this? This ain't nothing, but ten or twelve stacks," Skalez estimated, thumbing through the money by looking at it. Then he threw it in the bag, ran towards Lance and kicked him in the jaw with his black leather ACG boots. "You think this a muthafucking game, nigga?" He started to yell, taking the big bag strap from across his head. "I got something for your ass." He flipped Lance over on his back.

"Please don't do me dirty!" Lance cried.

"Didn't I say that if you lie to me again, I'll put this taser to your nuts?" Skalez pulled Lance's pants down to his ankles. Before Lance could utter a word, he tased his ball sacks. *Yinngg! Yinggg!*

"Great balls ah fire!" Block yelled and started laughing.

When Skalez let up, Lance started peeing on himself and holding his nuts while still handcuffed.

"Ah shit, look at this nigga. We should've bought some pampers with us," Block said, still laughing.

"Now where the fuck is the money?" Skalez asked, then tased him again for a couple more seconds.

Lance sat there sobbing quietly, still grabbing his balls not saying a word.

"Oh yeah, we been here before. The quiet game, huh? I brought something just for that," Skalez said, reaching in the bag and pulling out pliers. "I'ma ask you one more time before I put these pliers to one of your nuts and bust 'em. It's gonna be nut juice all over this mu'fucker."

"Th—th—that's all I got here." Lance started stuttering and slobbing.

"That's all you got, huh?" Skalez said through his teeth, grabbing his sack of balls and putting the teeth of the pliers around his left testicle squeezing it.

"Arghhhh! Shit!" Lance screamed out in pain and started crying. Block turned his head and squeezed his balls like it was his.

Skalez stood up, looking down on him. Lance couldn't do anything but scream and cry while his pants were down to his ankles. As he did that, he started to bleed from his pee hole. His left nut was literally busted and leaking.

"Now, I'ma ask you one more time. Where the fuck is the money?"

"It's—it's in my bedroom," he stuttered, tired of the pain.

"Which room is yours?"

"At the end of the hallway to the left."

Block grabbed both of his legs and dragged him into the hallway and to the room following Skalez.

"Where the fuck is it?" Skalez yelled.

"Behind the bookshelf over there."

Skalez looked at it, then walked over and pushed it away from the wall. He then stepped back to see the built-in volt. As he looked at the safe, he noticed it was three times bigger than the one in his office.

"Now that's what I'm talking 'bout. What's the combo?

"Please don't kill me after this. Man, please," Lance cried.

"Man, what the fuck is it? Ain't nobody going to kill you. That's my word. You wouldn't have got one of your balls busted if you just cooperated. Now what is it?" Skalez said.

Lance sighed. "9, 25, 9."

When the door opened to the built in safe in the wall, a big smile crept across his face. Block saw it from the side of his face and yelled, "Jackpot!"

"Yeah, jackpot for real," Skalez said, looking at the money that was stacked up. Skalez slowly turned around and pulled the gun out of his waist.

"I thought you said you wasn't going to kill me." Lance started to shake and cry.

"I lied. It's not like you never lied to get what you wanted before and stop crying. This shit part of the game. You knew what the rules were before you picked up and dribbled the ball. Your offense is cool, but your defense sucks. So here, hold these—" he said before he shot him three times in his chest.

*Bong, Bong, Bong!*

Followed by two more shots to the head from Block.

*Pop! Pop!*

"Let's get the money and get the fuck outta here," Skalez said.

While Skalez was throwing stack.after stack in the bag, Block was roaming through Lance's room.

"Damn, look at these Presidential Rolex watches," Block said, grabbing them. Opening the drawers of the dressers, he also saw two twin Mack 11s. "Well look at these shits," Block said, picking them both up in the air. "I'm glad this nigga didn't break free and make it over here."

Skalez turned around and looked across the huge bedroom to see what he was talking about.

"Yeah, I gotta get one of them and one of the Rolexes. Aye yo, we need at least two more bags," Skalez said, as Block walked towards the walk-in closet.

Opening the sliding door to the closet, he looked around and saw nothing but designer clothes. Then he said, "Bingo." He grabbed two Louis Vuitton traveling bags and brought it back out to Skalez.

"Yeah, they'll work," Skalez told Block who came on the side of him with the bags.

After they packed up the rest of the money, they went outside to the van and threw the three bags of money in the back. Then Skalez grabbed the gas can that was in the front on the floor and went back inside while Block started up the van, waiting for him.

As Skalez went back upstairs to where Lance, he dumped gas all over his body, then all over the room. Striking two matches at the same time, he threw them on the corpse. He watched Lance's body go up in flames as his face had a big Joker smile on it.

Then he ran out the house and hopped in the van where Block was waiting. Pulling out the long driveway, Skalez turned around and saw the fire moving throughout the house.

"We did it, fam," Block said with a smile.

"Yeah, we did," Skalez replied. "Let me call 40 real quick." He pulled out his cell phone and dialed the other burner number.

"Damn, it took y'all long enough to touch down," 40 said through the phone.

"It don't matter how long, we scored though. Y'all at the hotel?" Skalez asked.

"Yeah, it's just me and Tashia."

"Did y'all start counting that paper yet?

"Yeah and still counting."

"Well, that's always a good thing. But look, me and Block on our way."

"A'ight."

When Skalez got off the phone, he looked at Block. "What you laughing at? Skalez asked him.

"About how you became the nutcracker back there," Block said, laughing.

When the Streets Clap Back

# Chapter 13

As Skalez walked in the room, he looked at all the money stacked across the bed and table. Block came in behind him with a bag, shutting the door to the hotel room.

"Yeah, that's real good," Skalez said, smiling with a bag across his shoulders and another bag of money in his other hand.

"What's the count so far?" Block asked, dropping his bag on the floor.

"It's $195, 250 so far," Tashia replied. "I never thought I'd say this, but I'm tired of counting money."

"You tired of counting money? Well, we got three more bags to count over here." Skalez dropped two bags of money on the side of the bed, and sighed. "Shit, I ain't trying to count all this all night."

"Don't Wallo got a money counter?" 40 asked.

"Oh yeah, he damn sure do, don't he? Good thinking," Skalez said to 40, pulling his phone out to call his cousin.

Wallo answered on the fourth ring. "Who the fuck is this?" He was mad that someone woke him up from his sleep.

"This Skalez, nigga."

Wallo looked at the clock on his nightstand. "Nigga, it's 2:15 in the got damn morning."

"Yeah, I know, but I need a favor from you."

"And what is that?"

"I need to see your money counter."

"Oh yeah? What's in it for me?"

"God damn, nigga. You always want something."

"Shit, it seems like *you* always want something," Wallo shot back.

"I got something for you, but damn, we supposed to be cousins," complained Skalez.

109

"That's what I'm talking about. Family supposed to be looking out for family. So, look out, cousin."

"Yeah, a'ight. But look, you remember Tashia, right?

"You talking about that thick little chick you used to fuck with that went crazy after y'all broke up?"

"Yeah, yeah, her. She gonna be coming to get that and drop something off for you. Just look out for her in about fifteen or twenty minutes."

"That's cool."

"A'ight, I'm out." Skalez hung up and turned to Tashia. "Ay, go get that counter from Wallo on 26th street."

"I know where he lives." Tashia hopped right up.

"Take a stack and give it to him."

"Damn, why you giving that nigga that much?" 40 asked, looking at Skalez crazy.

"Fam, that shit ain't nothing compared to what we got and what your ass give away on tricking, you trick ass nigga." Skalez clowned him.

"Y'all niggas crazy." Tashia laughed.

"Anyway, Tashia, hurry up back," said Skalez.

"Nigga, don't be rushing me. I'll get back when I get back." She walked out of the door.

"You know what I just was thinking?" Block said, sitting on the bed next to the money.

"What's that?" asked 40, smiling.

"That nigga Wallo got a money counter, but don't got no cash to count." Block laughed at his own joke.

\*\*\*

While Skalez, 40 and Block sat waiting on Tashia to get back, they started smoking and talking about what they planned to do with their share of the money.

"I'ma chill for a minute, fall back and get on some business shit. I don't know what venture I'ma take, but with this money, I got options. Shit, I'm just a Crocket Street nigga just trying to get legit," Skalez said seriously as the weed was hitting him.

"I can feel that, but I'm trying to take a trip down to Miami for a week or two," Block proclaimed.

"Nigga, shut up and pass the blunt, Hoover ass nigga." 40 reached for the blunt.

"You know you two gonna be uncles, right?" Skalez just came out and said. 40 and Block looked at him with the stupid face.

"Huh, for real?" 40 said.

"Who the mother?" Block asked. Skalez looked at Block like he was crazy.

"You know it's Paula, you dumb ass nigga," Skalez laughed.

"Man, you a retarded ass nigga. You gotta be dumbest person Jesus Christ died for. You know Paula got that nigga pussy whipped," 40 joked.

"But yeah," Skalez said slowly, gazing off. "I'm about to be a father now. So now I gotta take precaution at whatever I do. I'ma use this money to invest in something that I know I will triple instead of blowing it on some bullshit."

"I got to be there for my child. We all grew up fatherless. Shit, the streets was our father. That's who raised us and I'll be damn if I don't be there for my seed. We all needed guidance, but didn't have it, so what we do? We went to the streets and got it the only way we knew how. I mean my mother taught me how to be a good individual and all, but she couldn't teach me how to be a man. I am who I am, but now I'm about to change because it's necessary."

40 and Block just sat there listening to Skalez vent.

"Look what the streets did to my older brother. He died by a bullet in the head. Look what they did to my cousin Dre! The Feds took him away and now his two girls gotta get raised like we did, fatherless. I'm just saying, I'm switching cycles up and kicking back on this to raise my child on some family shit. Sometimes when you see a way out, you gotta take it. They say life is like chess, so make your next move your best move and me, that's my best move. Man, take this shit from me," Skalez said, passing the blunt of weed. "Because I'm talking too much right now."

"You speaking some real shit, though! I got tired of hearing my father say he coming to my birthday or he'll be there for Christmas and never show up," 40 recalled.

"Damn, you all gon' make a thug cry. Fam, fuck all that father shit. I shot at my pops before. Fuck that nigga! That family shit is cool, though. But only for you. Me, I'ma bachelor. You know how Young Jezzy say, 'Trap or Die'. Well, for me it's 'Fuck or Die'. I'ma free agent, baby," Block said, laughing and choking on the weed.

"Block, I swear you the dumbest nigga I know," Skalez said, laughing. When Tashia made it back to the room, they started counting the rest of the money.

"Aye, your cousin Wallo is a wild guy," Tashia said, looking up with money in her hand still counting.

"What makes you say that?" Skalez asked, putting some hundred-dollar bills in the money counter.

"That nigga answered the door in some tight, little ass boxer briefs. Them shits was so small, I thought the nigga stole a pair of my boy shorts." All of them started laughing.

"Yeah, that nigga wild!" Skalez laughed because he knew Wallo was probably trying Tashia.

About two hours later, they totaled up all the cash up quicker with the money counter. They knew they could've used at least one more money counter, but they made up for it counting by hand.

The total was one million two hundred and fifty thousand dollars. Money was all over the room in twenty thousand stacks, so they knew what was what. The fifties were with the fifties and the hundreds were with the hundreds.

"Damn, this shit feels like we hit the lottery," 40 said, smiling as he looked at all the money on the floor, bed and table.

"Looking at all this money, I'm thinking it's fake," Tashia said excitedly.

"I'm just glad that this nigga had only fifties and hundreds 'cause if he had a lot of small bills, we literally would've been still counting it all," Skalez said, sitting on the bed.

"No bullshit," Block added on the floor, stacking the money up.

"This nigga had a quarter mil' at the stash house and exactly one million at his house. Something telling me this nigga had more. I know he did." Skalez mused, looking at all the money around him.

"A'ight, let's do the division on this." Skalez rubbed his hands together. "We got one million two hundred and fifty thousand dollars in the pot. Soooo—," Skalez said, dividing it in his head before he was cut off.

"So that's three hundred and twelve thousand dollars apiece," Tashia said, doing the math quickly in her head and smiling at Skalez.

"Damn, when it comes to dividing that money up, you sure know how to count fast. But when it's time to give up some pussy, you be acting dumb and slow," cracked Block.

"Nigga, whatever!" Tashia rolled her eyes.

"Who said you getting the same cut as us?" Skalez asked.

"Shit, y'all niggas ain't about to treat me like Lil BJ. Shit, I put in my work, too," Tashia said, pointing her finger at all of them, "Y'all didn't have to suck his little ass dick and fuck him."

"Naw, I'm just fucking with you, baby girl. As a matter of fact, you can keep the extra stack that's the odd," Skalez said, smiling but really was laughing about how she sucked his dick for it. *People will do anything for that dollar,* he thought.

"Thank you," she replied and smiled, getting up and kissing him on the cheek.

"Shit, that extra stack ain't no odds. We gonna divide that shit up, too. That's two hundred and fifty dollars a piece. You shouldn't have given that other thousand to Wallo," Block said, looking at Skalez.

"Nigga, shut up and let shorty keep the money," 40 said, picking up a stack of hundreds, throwing it at Block's head.

As they split the money four ways, Skalez was contemplating about his future with his girl and his soon to be new born child. *At least money wouldn't be an issue as of now,* he thought.

As he took a deep breath, he thought about the things people would do for money. *People will die for it. People will lie for it. People will kill for it. Shit, people will do the unthinkable for that paper, the power of the dollar. But we all need it to survive either way you look at it and I'm not trying to be struggling no more. I've been so far down before, that when I looked down, I still saw the bottom. It's like once you get the money, it don't fascinate you anymore. The struggle is what defines the individual, but when you get and make that money, it's all about what you do to maintain it and keep it flowing.*

A lot was going through Skalez's mind. He knew he had family to feed and look after, so he had to put it up for a rainy day. He knew Block and 40 were going to blow their money fast, but hoped they would do something positive with it.

"Damn, we done." Skalez zipped up his bag.

"Yeah, we had a long day for real." 40 yawned.

"Shit, I ain't tripping. A long day turned into some long money." Block stood up and throwing the duffle bag strap across his shoulder.

"If I had a bottle, I would drink to that," Tashia said, looking at Skalez's bag. "That Louie traveling bag is cute, too. Let's switch."

"Damn, you want everything, don't you? You know better than to ask me," Block said, looking at her like she was stupid. "You can get all the cute shit that you want now."

"Y'all ready to be out?" Skalez asked, quickly playing Tashia to the left.

"Yeah, let's ride," Block said.

Before walking out the door, Skalez stopped them. "Ay look, before we step foot out this door, nobody knows nothing," Skalez said, mainly looking and speaking to Tashia.

He knew she had a track star mouth, but her word was good. Plus, they'd been through this numerous times, but he still felt he had to say it.

"Fuck type of games you playing? Fuck I look like? Some kind of rat or something?" Block asked, looking at Skalez.

"Naw, nigga. You know I just had to put that out there," Skalez said, looking at Block.

"Let's get up outta here," Skalez said, walking out of the door.

Jibril Williams

# Chapter 14

Lil BJ was still feeling a little heated about how Skalez handled him in front of his crew. Then they only gave him five thousand dollars out the deal, especially when he saw 40 come out the house with 2 bags of money.

*It's cool. I didn't do much anyway,* he thought. *Let me call Bugg real quick,* Lil BJ said to himself in his room.

"Hello," Bugg answered on the third ring.

"Yo, what's good, fam? This is BJ."

"Who, Lil BJ?"

"Yeah, I need to holla at you about something."

"Well talk then 'cause time is money."

"You straight?" Lil BJ asked, trying to be discreet, but feeling the vibe that Bugg didn't care about him being discreet.

"Yeah, why? What'cha want? A quarter ounce again?"

"Naw, I need four and a baby."

"Oh yeah? You moving up, huh? You know I'm on 36th street, right?" Bugg said, meaning three thousand six hundred dollars.

"I already know. I'm trying to see you now, so where you at?"

"I'm on 24th. You still on 36th street, right?"

"Yeah, meet me at Leon's," Lil BJ said.

"You know I'm beefing with them niggas that be at the store. Just meet me on 35th and Madison in 5 minutes."

"Alright. Just bring your scale," Lil BJ said and hung up.

Lil BJ grabbed his 38 Snubnose and put it in his right pocket, then his flight jacket. Heading down the stairs, he saw his mother watching TV with her Saturday boyfriend because she damn sure had one for every day of the week.

"Where you think you going at 11:30 at night?" his mother said to him.

He paid her no mind and went straight out the door. She knew she couldn't tame him and didn't even try to come behind him either. When he got outside on the porch of the apartment, he saw his sister and her friend smoking weed.

"Let me hit that real quick," BJ said.

"Hell naw! You always wanna smoke somebody shit up," his sister Vanessa said.

He looked at her for a quick second, then at her friend Trici who started laughing.

"Well fuck both y'all bitches then," he said, taking the blunt out her hand and throwing it before ran.

As she got up, she ran after the blunt instead of him, thinking it went in the puddle of water. As he made it around the corner to 35th and Madison, he saw Bugg's late model Lexus.

"What's good?" Lil BJ said, getting into the car.

"This paper," Bugg replied.

"That's all and what it's gon' to be. So where the scale and weight at?

"Where dat cash at?" Bugg smiled, showing his mouth full of golds. Lil BJ went into his pocket and pulled out a knot of money.

"Here's that thirty-six right here," Lil BJ said, passing the money already counted up.

"I like to see a nigga stepping up," Bugg said, grabbing the money. Reaching under the seat, he grabbed the Ziplock bag.

"Get the scale out the glove compartment. I'ma count this money up while you weighing that shit."

\*\*\*

Walking back to his crib with four and a half ounces of coke in his boxer briefs made him feel a whole lot better, coming from where he came from, which was nothing.

*I just ain't have a penny to my name. Now, I got this and the fourteen hundred at the crib. Skalez could've looked out more, but shit, I can't complain,* Lil BJ thought to himself. Making it back to the apartment, his sister and her friend were nowhere in sight. Neither was his mother. He went upstairs to his room, shut the door and picked up the cordless house phone. *First things first, I gotta pay my cell phone bill,* he thought, while making a call on the phone.

"Yo, who this?" Lil Chris asked, answering the phone.

"What's up, fam?"

"Nigga, where you been? I been calling your cell phone and that shit off. And when I call your crib, your sister be hanging up on a nigga. What's up with that shit?"

"Yeah, I just told myself I gotta pay that cell bill. It got turned off earlier, but check it, I got something for you tomorrow."

"What is it?"

"Don't worry about it. Just know we straight for now."

"I hope it's some cash 'cause a nigga damn sure need some."

"It's something to get us some cash and more than what a nigga been pushing

"Oh yeah? I feel you."

"How is your leg doing?"

"It's cool. Them niggas didn't slow shit down. But I swear the next time I run across that nigga with my brother chain on, I'ma send that nigga on to the Most High."

"I feel you and I'm with you, my nigga. Just know you got another brother right here," Lil BJ said, being sincere.

"No doubt. I already know."

"Ah look, I'm getting off the phone. Just come by the crib tomorrow with your cripple ass," Lil BJ said, laughing.

"Nigga, I can still drive."

"I know. I'ma holla at you tomorrow," Lil BJ told him and hung up, looking at the work on the bed. "It's not a lot for a lot of people, but it's a start for me," he said out loud to himself.

# Chapter 15

Six months had passed and things had changed tremendously for everybody. Skalez hadn't pulled a caper since Lance nor looked back since then. He couldn't speak for his boys, 40 and Block, though. They went on different routes, but the money stayed flowing steadily like a faucet for them all.

Skalez and Paula moved into a gated community called Farmington out in Hampton, Virginia. Paula was now seven months pregnant. Skalez made her submit her request to go on leave at the hospital. She didn't want to, feeling capable to work. They argued back and forth about that situation before finally she gave in. Skalez just didn't want to chance her hurting herself and the baby.

She thought he was being over protective, but he cared too much for her to take a chance. He went to all her doctor appointments and Lamaze classes he could make. The money stayed coming because of his barbershop, Fresh To Death Outs, and his beauty and nail salon, Heavenly Fashion Beauty and Nail Salon he had just opened.

It started out slow, but now the businesses were booming. The barbershop and beauty and nail salon were right next door to each other, so it was convenient for couples. But there was only one problem. It was right in the hood.

One time a fight broke out and someone started shooting right out front. A bullet came through the window hitting someone. But the money was always rolling in at a good pace, so they stayed.

Skalez's cousin Raymond just got home after a 5-year bid, so Skalez gave him letting him run the barbershop whenever he wasn't there. Plus, he could cut hair. This was as plus since he didn't want to see his cousin go back to prison, keeping him close so he would stay out of trouble.

He wanted Paula to run the hair and nail salon, but he didn't want her in the hood late at night. Not when anything was liable to happen. So, he let his mother run it since they were from the bottom of Bad News and used to be in the business.

He always told Paula they were just going to sit back and collect the money. In fact, the only time Skalez showed his face was to collect the weekly payment.

"Speak on it," Skalez said, answering his phone.

"What's good, cuzzo?" his cousin Raymond said.

"Ain't shit. Just moving through traffic. Why, what's up?"

"You coming by the shop today?"

"I'm on my way to the salon to get my shit twisted now. What's on your mind?"

"I just need holla at you about something."

"A'ight, give me uhh," Skalez said, looking at his watch, "about 20 minutes."

"Ok, cool. I'll see you then."

While Skalez was cruising down Toad's Lane, he called 40.

"Who this?" 40 said, picking up his phone like he had a problem.

"Damn, playboy. Where the love at?" Skalez said, playing with his partner in crime.

"My fault, fam. This bitch keep blowing a nigga phone up on some fatal attraction shit. I knew I shouldn't have put that King Kong on that bitch," 40 said, while Skalez started laughing. "But anyway, what's good, fam?" 40 asked him.

"I'm just checking on you, fam. You talk to Block lately?"

"Yeah, I talked to that nigga last night."

"I called that nigga twice and I didn't get an answer."

"You know he laid up with Christy somewhere. That nigga fell in love with a stripper, T-Pain ass nigga," 40 said, laughing at his own joke

"No bullshit. Rick James and Teena Marie ass nigga."
Skalez laughed with 40. "A'ight, a'ight, a'ight," Skalez said,
yelling through the phone as he tried to stop laughing.

"What you 'bout to do?" 40 asked.

"I'm 'bout to go holla at Raymond at the shop and get
my hair braided."

"Shit! I should swing through there. I need to get my shit
cut, too."

"Come on through. I'ma be in the salon getting my shit
twisted."

"What you getting, some straight back joints?"

"Nigga you know I don't do the plain Jane shit," Skalez
said, being cocky. "Only designer, fam."

"Yeah, right you. Fake Allen Iverson ass nigga."

"Nigga, you crazy. He's the homie and all, but A.I. ain't
got shit on me. But look, I'm pulling at the shop. Just holla
at me when you come down the bottom."

"A'ight."

"A'ight, fam," Skalez said and hung the phone up.

As Skalez got out his new 2007 QX 56 truck on Chestnut
Avenue in front of both the shops, he saw a familiar face out
front just lingering around.

"What's good, Skalez?" the dude said. Skalez just nodded his head and entered the barbershop. Stepping inside, he
heard Jim Jones' "Balling" coming from the speakers
throughout the shop.

"What's good, boss man?" one of the barbers spoke, then
the rest of them acknowledged him.

"Ain't nothing, fellas. I see it's packed in here today,"
Skalez said, looking around.

"What day it ain't?" one of barbers shot back at Skalez.

"Yeah, it's a good thing," Raymond said, coming from
the back. As he he approached Skalez, he dapped him up.
Then they both went to the office in the back of the shop.

"What you need to holla at me about?" Skalez said, shutting the door behind him and getting straight to the point.

"A'ight, look. I wanted to get your permission first before I do this—" Raymond started to say before he was cut off by Skalez.

"No, it ain't happening," Skalez said firmly.

"You don't even know what I was going to say," Raymond told him with his arms out.

"Just the way you started it off, it sounds funny."

"Let me finish first," Raymond said.

"A'ight, I'm all ears." Skalez waited, crossing his arms.

"Ok, listen. I got some serious weight right now that I need—" Raymond started to say again, but got cut off.

"Nigga, hell naw!" Skalez yelled. "Nigga, you crazy? This is where I make my bread and butter. My place of business is not no damn stash spot. Nigga, your aunt and my mother, is right next door.

"This shit is crazy. You're older than me and I'm the one acting like I got all the sense. Cousin, I gave you a job so you can stay out of trouble and dodge the bullshit. You are going to fuck around and be back right behind them bars you just came from."

"But this shit can benefit the both of us," Raymond argued.

Skalez looked at him seriously with murder in his eyes. "You don't get it, do you?" Skalez said slowly. "I want you to listen up closely. I don't care if your ass is family, if you cross me or go against me, on my word I'll drop your body off on a corner like a two-dollar trick. Now get back to work or get the fuck out my shop." He walked out, leaving him there with an angry face.

\*\*\*

Entering the beauty and nail salon was a lot different than going into the barbershop. Men got an eye full of all the eye candy that worked there and the female customers coming and going. The setup of the shop was professional with a woman's touch, and like most female businesses, there was alwaysa bunch of gossiping that went on. Especially since the salon is in the hood.

"Hey, sweetie. Come give your momma a kiss," Skalez mother said to him as he came in the salon.

Everybody called his mother, Momma Mona, even the hustlers around there. She always gave motherly advice and love to everyone. Skalez didn't mind showing his mother some love whenever or wherever, but he always hated that make-up he got on his shirt whenever he hugged her. As he hugged and kissed her, he noticed Tashia sitting in a chair getting her hair done.

"Well, well," Skalez said, walking over to Tashia after leaving his mother. "You got a little money and act like you don't know a brother no more, huh?" As she looked up, she realized it was Skalez talking to her.

"Naw, it ain't never like that, pretty boy. I just been busy," she replied, looking at Skalez up and down, taking in his tall slim frame, then smiled.

Truthfully, she was really hurt that Paula was having his child. Even though she had two kids of her own, she still had hope that Skalez would come back and be in a relationship with her, but it never happened.

"Damn, it's been like what, eight months now?" Skalez said, sitting down in the chair next to Tashia to get his hair braided.

"You know I just moved. I'm still trying to get everything in order. "

"What you trying to get today?" the hairdresser asked Skalez.

"You know what I like, so just do you, baby girl," Skalez replied.

"Hey, Jermaine. I'm about to run out for a while. You gonna be here when I return?" Skalez's mother asked him from across the room.

"Yeah, if I'm not finish getting my hair done."

"Well, if you don't, momma loves you, baby," she said and walked off towards the door.

"Love you, too." He watched his mother walk out the salon.

"Ahhhh, that's so sweet," Tashia said. "Your momma still looking good, but I know she is still crazy."

"You better watch what you say about my momma," Skalez warned her, grinning.

"How is Paula coming along?" Tashia asked kind of slow, looking directly in to his eyes.

"She's cool. Just poking out a little."

"So, what y'all having?"

"We are having a girl," Skalez disclosed with a smile.

"Uh oh," Tashia said, giggling. "Time to bring the guns back out."

"Congratulations," Felicia, the hair dresser, said.

"Thank you," Skalez replied.

"You pick out a name yet?" Tashia asked, sitting beside Skalez before she got to leave since her hair was done.

"Yeah, we came up with a couple. Well, really me. Paula let me pick out the names, but I like Talaya and Janiyah."

"Those names are cute," Tashia said, brushing he hair over her shoulder with her right hand. "Well look, Skalez. I got to run."

"Okay, Tashia. Take it easy."

"Tell Paula I said congratulations and take care."

"Will do. Just make sure you start answering your phone. We still friends, aren't we?"

"Of course. If it wasn't for your help, I wouldn't be where I am today," she said, pulling out keys to her brand-new Benz truck from her Gucci hand bag.

"It's mutual," he said, knowing where she was coming from.

"I'ma get with you later," she said and walked out the door.

One of the hairdressers that was eavesdropping on their conversation told her client, "I think them two used to fuck around."

"Uh hm. You can tell by the way she sounded so sad when they were talking about the baby," the client replied.

Jibril Williams

# Chapter 16

Block had been laid up in the condo a lot lately with Christy. He had made her his main woman now and felt nothing but good vibes from being around her. It wasn't just because the sex was good. She was educated, too. She was different from a lot of the other chicks he was used to dealing with. His boys made jokes and comments about it, but he paid them no mind. A lot had changed for Block since the robbery with Lance. He switched from robbing the major dope boys in the city to becoming a major dope boy himself. He was knee deep in the game, him and his boy, 40. Skalez, well he really didn't indulge with his friends on that level. He was on his legit business shit.

Christy hit the button on the wall in kitchen to talk to get his attention.

"Hey, baby. The food is ready," she said through the intercom that could be heard on the third-floor level of the condo.

"A'ight, I'm on my way down," Block replied from the game room. He was looking at ESPN, smoking some weed. "Damn, this shit is good," he said, inhaling the smoke, then looked at the blunt.

*Ain't nothing like that morning high.*

As he reached the bottom level of their crib, he went and sat down at the glass dining room table. He put the blunt of out in the ashtray he had, then threw it to his all-white pit bull he named Snow.

"That's why Snow is always looking like he's ready to pass out," Christy said, placing his plate of food in front of him.

"Shit, he be begging for it. You should've seen the way he was looking at me and following me around," Block replied, picking up his fork and digging into his food.

"Dude, you are crazy." She shook her head.

"Why you always feeding a nigga turkey sausage and shit? Girl, I ain't Muslim. I love me some pork and you being with me, you gon' love some pork, too," Block told her, putting jam on his toast.

"Boy, you know I don't eat no pork," Christy said, sitting down with her plate.

"I can't tell. You eat my pork every night," he teased her, laughing.

"Oh, you funny now, huh?"

"Naw, baby, but for real—" Block started to say before he swallowed his food. "You can cook to be a white girl. You season your shit just right."

"Oh, you think that white people can't cook?"

"Well, I thought so until I met you. You know white people shit always be plain."

When they were done eating, Christy picked up their plates and took them to the kitchen.

"I'ma need you to deliver two joints to Keith today," Block said, standing to his feet following her.

"Damn, he done with that other shit already?"

"Yeah, they loving that new shit I got from Miami."

"Where do you want me to meet him at? The same spot or at the club tonight?"

"Take it to the spot around 2 o'clock," he said.

Block had been using Christy as his drop off and pick up person. People really would not expect it, with her being white and all. Block and 40 used the same connect, but they had their own operations as to how they went about their business.

"I'm about to head to the shower and get ready for the day," Block said, getting ready to walk off.

"What you got planned for today?"

"Spending some cash. I might get another chin to add to the one I got. I'ma head to the mall after that, then to Fresh to Death Cuts to get a line up."

"You know it's good that your boy opened those shops and laid back with his family from the streets," she said, putting it out there with hopes that Block would catch the hint and he chill from the streets.

"Yeah, I'm happy for him and glad he's out the streets, but me—Well, I'm stuck to the streets like dirt on concrete."

After Block took his shower, he got dressed throwing on a red and white striped Polo Shirt, blue Polo jeans and some red and white Prada shoes. He looked at himself in the full mirror on the back of his walk-in closet, then he went in to see what he was looking for.

"A nigga feel lost without this," he said as he took his VA fitted cap off his hat rack, putting it on his head with the brim low, barely over his eyes. He then walked out and grabbed his long 42-inch gold Cuban link chain with the big gold Jesus piece attached to it and threw it over his head. Then he headed out the door, not even telling Christy he was leaving.

"Talk to me, I talk back," Block said, answering his phone while driving.

"How's the married life treating you?" Skalez teased.

"Who me? Naw you must have dial the wrong number."

"Naw, I got the right number, Mr. Bachelor, that's been playing house with Ms. Wonder Bread."

"I know your ass ain't talking, family man."

"Yeah, yeah, but where you been nigga? I been calling you for the last couple of days."

"I been really busy in these streets, fam. Shit been moving so fast for me lately. I'm running a track relay race."

"Oh yeah? Well, that's always a good thing! Business is doing well, but you know a fast pace can be problem at times, also."

"Well, that's what I like! I'm in the fast line."

"Me, I'm in the slow lane. You can never go wrong with taking your time. You always get better results and as long as that money coming in, I'm good. I can't complain, even if it's at a slow pace. But when it's not coming in at all, that's when I get worried and niggas need to watch themselves," Skalez said seriously through the phone.

"I feel that. It sounds good, too."

"It doesn't just sound good, try it. It feels good, especially when you ain't got to look over your shoulders. One thing I know is that there is always someone else out there wishing they were in your position. So they will try to take what you gotta get, to be where you are at all cost. You know how the game goes."

"Yeah, you right! You think your ass know everything, too."

"Naw, fam. A fool think he knows everything, but really don't know shit. But I do know a little of a lot. You can bet that. But I am content with what I got and happy where I'm at in life."

"I'm glad you are 'cause I damn sure ain't!"

"Well, you better learn to value this shit. But anyway, what you about to get into?" Skalez asked, changing the subject. He knew Block was going to do whatever he wanted to do, not taking heed on anything, but what he felt was right.

"I'ma 'bout to head uptown to Patrick Henry Mall real quick and get a few things. Maybe add to this jewelry I got."

"Yeah, that's crazy you still got that chain."

"What you expect? It's mine. Why wouldn't I have it? Where you at, though?"

"I'm about to leave the shop right now. I just got my shit twisted."

"Oh yeah? I was gonna swing through there and get a line up after I leave from Uptown."

"Just hit me up before you come back down to the bottom. 40 over here with me, too. We about to make a run real quick, so just hit me up, a'ight?"

"A'ight, fam," Block said and hung up the phone.

As Block entered the mall, he didn't know which way to turn. The mall for him was like a fat kid in a candy store. He just went crazy and hyper. He stopped at Footlocker first and copped two pair of the new Jordans they had on display through the window.

After he left there, he went into the Gucci store and went crazy, walking out with four bags and the two he had from Footlockers. He started walking down the mall strip until he saw what he was looking for.

As he entered the jewelry store, he started looking at all the pieces that were on display. Amyir, the owner, was well known throughout the Virginia area. He had customized pieces for the likes of Allen Iverson, Marcus Vick, and Pusha-T from the rap group Eclipse and upcoming rapper, Fanes, just to name a few.

Now that Block was able to ball out the way he wanted to, he did what bosses did and that's customize everything. As he looked around the store, a well-dressed middle-aged black man came from the back wearing a suit. "May I help you with anything?" he asked.

"Yeah, well you actually can," Block said, looking at the man.

"Okay, what is it that you are interested in? Do you like anything you see?"

"Kinda sorta, but I would like to get something made."

"Oh, I see. Well in that case, let me get Mr. Amyir," the salesman said and walked into the back of the store.

Block sat his bags down in front of one of the glass display cases, looking at a nice diamond tennis bracelet. He immediately thought of Christy.

His thoughts were broken when a young, black guy that looked to be in his mid-20s approached him.

"What's up? How can I help you today?" Amyir, the jeweler asked, greeting Block with a handshake.

Amyir came out in some jeans, a white T-shirt and some all-white Air Forces. It's crazy how the salesman came out all suited up while Amyir came out in jeans and Nikes. Well, you know the saying. It costs to be the boss. With Amyir, it seemed to have paved the way for him to be comfortable in his own place of business. When he came out, Block shook his hand.

"Yeah, I'm looking to get something made."

"I like the chain that you got on. It looks like it was custom made, also," Amyir said, admiring Block's chain.

"Yeah, with the way I rock it, it was made for me, huh?" Block said with a smile.

Amyir smiled along with Block. "I like your style and designing pieces are my specialty. So, what is the visual you see that you want me to bring to life?"

Entering into Amyir's office he had pictures of his jewelry work. They sat down and talked about the pieces Block wanted. Amyir pulled out a fat joint of weed, rolling it in white paper.

"You smoke?" Amyir asked. Block was shocked that he felt so comfortable around a total stranger.

"Do I? Hell yeah, I smoke!" Block replied, smiling. They smoked the joint while discussing the piece and prices. After they were done, Block pulled out a knot of one hundred-dollar bills, counted it out and gave it to Amyir.

"That's 15 thousand right there. I'll give you the rest when you are done." Amyir smiled with his eyes bloodshot red and glossy.

"I got you, Block, and thank you for choosing me as your jeweler. I'm definitely going to holla at you about the other business, also."

"No doubt. You also got some good ass hospitality, that goes a long way," Block said smiling, dapping Amyir up, then walked out his office leaving him behind.

Grabbing his bags, Keith, the salesman asked, "You got everything you were looking for?"

"Actually, naw. Let me get this diamond tennis bracelet over here," Block said, putting his bags back down as he walked and pointed at the bracelet he saw earlier.

"This one right here?" the salesman asked, grabbing it from inside of the case. "Who's the special lady? Is it for your girl?"

"I guess you can say that."

"Well, it's an all-around gift for any kind of woman, no matter the situation or occasion, so it's a perfect choice," he said, trying to hype it up for the sale. He then wiped the bracelet down and wrapped it up. It cost him $5,985.

Block pulled out another knot similar to what he had earlier. He handed him six grand, grabbed his gift for Christy and walked out the jewelry store. As he made his way to the food court, he stopped at Chow Chinese Spot. He got him some beef and broccoli and two egg rolls, choosing to eat at the mall. He was so into what he was doing, he failed to pay attention to his surroundings.

*** 

*That's that nigga right there,* Lil Chris said to himself, hyped with his adrenaline pumping as he passed Block in the food court.

"I won't fuck this up this time," he said, picking up his cell phone dialing a number. A couple rings later, someone answered.

"Yo, who this?"

"Listen, I need you to come to Patrick Henry Mall right now."

"Why, what's up?" the guy asked.

"Fam, just get here ASAP!" Lil Chris said and hung up.

***

Block held the cell phone to his ear. "I got a surprise for you tonight when I see you," he said.

"Oh yeah? What is it?" Christy asked a little too excited.

"Now you know damn well it won't be no surprise if I told you."

"Well, you shouldn't have told me then," Christy said, sounding disappointed.

"That's how you white girls are in the movies. Always wanting to know what's behind the door or something. Shit, even when y'all know something or someone is going to kill you. Then when y'all run, y'all always trip and fall or do some clumsy shit," Block joked.

"Well, if that's the case, why do black people always die first?" she asked.

"Now that's the shit I don't get. Knowing us black folks, we be getting the fuck out of dodge when shit be going down. I guess they don't want to see us make it. But anyway, let me get off this phone while I'm driving. You know how these cops are."

"Alright, baby. Be safe."

"Shit, that's my middle name. It can't get no safer than me. I'm gone," he said, disconnecting the call as he got on the interstate.

He called Skalez to let him know that he was on the way to the shop. While cruising through traffic, Block didn't realize he was being followed.

"What's good with you, ugly ass niggas," Block said, walking up on Skalez and 40 in front of the beauty and nail salon and barbershop.

"Man, you Shrek look alike ass nigga. You the only ugly person I see in my presence right now," 40 replied.

"Yeah, whatever, nigga. Well, I'm about to go inside Fresh to Death and get a cut real quick. As a matter of fact, look at me, nigga. This how money walks," Block said and walked off into the shop with his Diddy bop.

Skalez smiled to himself and shook his head at his two friends tripping. *Damn we have came along way,* he thought. They went from rags to riches, driving Honda Civics to pushing 5s and 6s.

Skalez started rapping to himself as he walked in behind 40 and Block. After Block was finished with his haricut, they went in the back of the barbershop and shot some pool in the game room. The room was mostly used for shooting dice whenever the neighborhood hustlers slid through.

They talked and kicked it for a while, talking about different ventures and how they wanted to further expand their business. But of course, they all had different approaches.

After they were done kicking it, they all departed ways. Block looked at his Rolex watch from Lance. *It's 5:37 p.m.,* he said to himself. As he hopped into his ride to head to his condo, he called Christy.

"What's good, Snow White?" Block asked when Christy answered the phone.

"Why you always calling me that?"

"It ain't hard to tell. It's because you're white and you look like a princess. Well, really more like a queen. Now, where you at?"

"I'm on my way to get my nails done," Christy replied.

"A'ight, well I'm on my way to the crib right now, but I'ma stop at Walmart first. So just holla at me later on when you done."

"Will do, sweetie."

"A'ight, Snow White," Block said and disconnected the call.

# Chapter 17

His vantage point was unobstructed, so he could clearly identify the man he sought. "That's him right there," Lil Chris said, pointing at the guy in the crowd walking out of the mall.

"Who?" Lil BJ asked, looking.

"The one with all the bags in the red and white striped shirt."

"I can't see his face good," Lil BJ told him, looking at whomever he was pointing at.

"Where you park?" Lil Chris asked.

"On the other side of Dillards."

"Well, I parked on this side. Just leave your car and we'll come back and get it in a few hours."

"A'ight."

As they walked to Lil Chris' car, Lil BJ told him he had saw that car before, but couldn't make it out where. As they followed his car down Chestnut Avenue, they parked four cars down from where he had parked his car.

When Lil BJ saw who had gotten out of the Lexus, his blood pressure rose.

"Oh shit!" Lil BJ said with a shocked look on his face.

"Oh shit, what?" Why you looking at him like that? You know him or something?" Lil Chris asked, looking at Lil BJ, then back at the guy walking across the street.

"Aye yo, fam. This shit is crazy," Lil BJ said, while watching Block walk across the street where Skalez and 40 were.

"Talk to me, nigga. What's up?"

"Aye, remember when I told you I went on a lick with some dude that used to fuck with my sister?" Lil BJ was still eyeing Block and them.

"Yeah, what about it?"

"It's that dude right there with the corn rolls, the tall one and his partners, 40 and Block. Block is the one with your brother's chain on. I heard Skalez had a beauty salon and barbershop, but I didn't know fo'show," Lil BJ said, watching the three of them walk in the barbershop. "They used to be on some serious stick up shit too, and their body count, I heard, is in the double digits."

"Fam, I don't see none of that shit. I'm about to catch me a couple of bodies, starting with this nigga right here with my brother chain on. You said they on some stick up shit, right?"

"Yeah."

"Well, shit. They probably the ones that got my brother and his crew. And if they weren't, I'm gonna make it feel like they were. You fuck with them niggas or something?"

"I did, but fam, I'm with you. We gonna get these niggas. I ain't like how that nigga Skalez tried to play me in front of them niggas anyway."

"We going to follow this nigga Block when he comes back out. You strapped?"

"Like an old pair of Filas! Nigga, you know I can't leave home without mines," Lil BJ said, pulling out a black 9-millimeter Berretta.

As they waited for them to come out of the barbershop, they discussed how they were going to get them all, but it would take some time. They knew Fresh To Death Cuts and Heavenly Fashion Salon was Skalez', so they knew where and how to get him at all times later down the road.

They were thinking about how they were going to catch 40, but really didn't have a plan on how to handle Block. Lil Chris was just excited that he finally saw him again and how he wanted to run up on him at close range the first chance he got.

Lil Chris and Lil BJ had been waiting an hour and a half when their patience finally paid off, watching Block and his crew leave headed in different directions.

Lil Chris then turned the engine on. Block had pulled off, cruising, not knowing his time to live was counting down.

"Let's ride on this nigga," Lil Chris said as they followed him.

# Chapter 18

On the way to his condo, he stopped at Walmart to get a couple of things. Block loved going into Walmart. It was like he was going into a mini mall because everyone would be up in there shopping. Walking to the food section where the cereal was located, he grabbed a box of CoCo Puffs.

*Gotta have these,* he said to himself and picked up two boxes, throwing them in his basket. Walking out of that section, he headed towards the beverages where he picked up a 24 pack of Corona before heading to one of the cash registers.

While waiting in line, he was looking at a girl's ass in front of him.

"Damn, that shit fat," he said to himself. As soon as he did, she turned around to see who was behind her and smiled.

After he left, he headed to his car to put his cereal and beer in the back seat with the other items he got earlier from the mall. Heading to his crib, he knew Christy probably wouldn't be back yet, so he decided to plan something for her to go with the bracelet he'd gotten her.

Reaching his condo, Block drove up to his personal parking spot. After getting out of his car, he closed the door and opened the back door to grab some of the bags. After putting them by the stairs, he turned around to get the rest when a figure smacked him in the face with a gun. Then he heard his front door close. When the other guy came towards him, Block saw his face and his eyes got big.

"You bitch ass nigga," was all Block got out before three bullets to the face snapped his head back and dropped him to the ground.

*Bow! Bow! Bow!* Three successful shots were delivered to him what he had so callously done to others.

"Nice chain you got on," said the killer, snatching it from around Block's neck right before the brazen jackboy took his last breath.

# Chapter 19

Christy felt that something wasn't right as she made her way to Block's condo. "Damn, why he's not answering his phone? That's not like him?" Christy mumbled to herself for the one hundredth time. Turning onto the street where his condo was, she saw nothing but police, paramedics and people standing around.

"Damn, what the fuck happened around here?" she asked herself as she slowly drove down the street.

Her stomach knotted up when she saw the paramedics coming out of Block's condo with a body. "Oh God! Please don't!" she screamed, stopping in the middle of the street and getting out of her car as she ran towards the condo.

When she approached the condo, one of the police officers grabbed her as she reached the yellow tape.

"Excuse me, Miss. Do you stay at this residentce or something?" the officer asked.

"No! I mean yes! This is my boyfriend's place," Christy said quickly with a worried look. "Who was the person that was brought out of the house?"

"If this is your boyfriend's place, then I would hate to tell you this but—"

"Oh God, no!"

"Your boyfriend was shot multiple times and died on the scene," the officer advised.

Christy started crying and yelling for a couple seconds before she passed out.

When she woke up, she looked around, not realizing where she was. She looked to her left and saw monitors. When she got out of the bed, she grabbed her Air Max sneakers off the ground and ran out the room barefoot.

"What am I going to do?" she kept saying to herself and crying.

Reaching the front of the hospital, she realized that she didn't have any money on her, a car or a cell phone. She looked around and saw a man on a cell phone and walked over to him.

"Excuse me, sir. Do you mind if I use your phone when you're done?"

The man looked at her like she was crazy if she thought he was going to let her use his prepaid phone. Then he softened up when he saw tears coming down her face.

"Hey, let me call you back," the man said, ending his call before he handed it to Christy. "Is everything all right?" the man asked.

"No, it's not," she said, dialing a number. "My boyfriend just died."

"I'm so sorry to hear that."

"Me, too," she replied, wiping her face with one hand. "Skalez, I need you to come to the hospital and get me."

"Who is this? Christy?"

"Yeah."

"What's up and why does it sound like you're crying?" he asked curiously.

"He—He—He died, Skalez! My baby died! He's gone," Christy stuttered.

"What? Who? Where?" Skalez yelled into the phone. He couldn't believe what Christy just said, but he wanted her to say it again just to be sure he heard her right.

"Block, Skalez! Block!" she screamed, then dropped to her knees crying.

"What hospital you at?"

"Sentera Hampton," she replied, still crying on her knees.

In fifteen minutes flat, Skalez, 40, Raymond and a couple more guys pulled up, four cars deep and hopped out.

"Christy, where the fuck Block at? What the fuck is going on?" Skalez barked.

"I told you, Skalez," she replied, her face beet red from crying.

Skalez fled past her and ran to the front desk in the hospital. "Is there an Alvin Johnson here?" he asked the lady behind the desk eating some cookies.

"Uhhhh, I think we brought a guy in by that name. Let me see," she said, munching on her cookie while typing on the computer. "Oh yes, here it is. Oh," she said slowly, looking back at him and the entourage he had behind him.

"Oh what? What is it? What do that fuckin' computer say?" Skalez braced himself for the worst.

"I probably shouldn't tell you this, but he was pronounced dead before he got here."

After she said that, Skalez looked at 40 and both of their minds went blank. 40 started to stare off in space. He was looking at Skalez, but really was looking through him. Skalez turned around and looked for Christy. When he saw her, she was sitting in the chair hugging herself, rocking back and forth crying. He then walked over to her.

"Christy, let me holla at you outside for a minute," Skalez said with the rest of them walking off behind him. He stopped. "Aye 40, you and the rest of y'all let me holla at shorty," Skalez said, dismissing the rest.

Skalez started interrogating her like she was a part of his death, but let up some once he saw how much she loved his boy than to do something like set him up.

"We got to find out who did this shit right now," 40 said angrily. "Go to his house and see if it was a robbery or what. We gotta find a fucking motive, fam. This shit hurt for real!" 40's voice was full of pain.

# Chapter 20

A month had passed since the death of Block and they still hadn't found the killer, or found out why he was killed. It wasn't a robbery, his boys concluded because he still had money in his stash and a couple of kilos in his condo. The funeral they had for him was nice. He went out in style. The ceremony was packed. It almost seemed like the whole city came out. Even Block's father, whom he had only seen twice in his life, had shown up.

Block's mother went off as soon as she saw him, but she eventually calmed down. People that Block, Skalez, and 40 didn't even know or socialize with, but saw in the hood, showed their faces as well to pay their last respect or just to see if Block was really dead or not.

Females that Block used to deal with were crying all during the ceremony. Christy felt bad, but held her head high throughout the whole thing. 40 sat in the front row, staring at the corpse in daze lost in his thoughts, while Skalez was in the back of the church looking at the faces that was in the room. He knew he and his crew hadn't dealt with 75% of the people in that church, but he kept his composure throughout the whole thing.

*You can be here today and gone tomorrow,* he thought as he looked towards the casket.

# Chapter 21

40 hadn't been the same since the passing of Block. He'd been drinking a lot and started to sniff his own work. He still kept his appearance up and the money kept coming in, but it's was like the more money came in, the more reckless he became about conducting his business.

He was no longer being cautious; he'd begun talking reckless on the phone, even taking everything for granted. Skalez tried to talk some sense into him, but 40 did what he wanted to do. He always said, *I do what the fuck I does.* Every time Skalez saw him, he was high on something or drunk.

"Damn, you need to get your shit together. A nigga don't like to see you like this," Skalez said, showing concern. 40 just looked at him from the passenger seat with his glassy eyes, high off the weed and cocaine.

"What you talking about, fam? My shit airtight and waterproof," 40 replied.

"Listen, 40. You the last brother that I got, fam, and I won't tell you nothing that's not good for you. I've been knowing you far too long not to know what's going on with you. I can see it in your eyes. You might look good to others with your appearance and all, but you look like shit to me. You stressing, fam. Just tighten up and get yourself together because sometimes when a person is stressing, he start slipping. You need to catch yourself before you go sliding down that ladder."

40 gazed out of the window as the rain fell on the glass while Skalez drove down Harpersville Road.

"I just miss my nigga, fam," 40 just came out and said slowly, sounding depressed. "It just haven't been the same without Block."

As 40 talked, Skalez just listened, allowing him to vent because he rarely did. He knew they all needed that one person that they could confide in.

"It's like the better shit gets, the worse it gets. You remember when we were 16 and snuck up in that strip club, Moonlight?" 40 replied, reminiscing.

"Yeah, I remember that shit. We got kicked out when that ugly ass bitch came on stage shaking her ass. Her legs looked like she had bullet wounds all on her thighs and ass cheeks," Skalez said, laughing along with 40.

"Yeah, yeah, yeah. And that crazy ass nigga Block reached in his pocket and pulled out a handful of change, making it rain quarters, nickels, and dimes."

Skalez was laughing so hard, he had to slow down while driving. "Damn, I miss my nigga," Skalez lamented. "Just know we got another Angel watching over us. The dead also be the ones to save our lives at times when them bullets get to flying. They are the ones that push them bullets past us when we know we were supposed to get hit by them."

"Yeah or them niggas can't shoot," 40 said, joking.

"But look, 40. All we got is us, fam." Skalez pulled over at 40's crib to drop him off. "And I'm not gonna see anything happen to you or see you doing bad. We all we got. I'll bust my gun for you until my palms get sore, then use the other hand. I love you, my nigga, before this paper. This shit ain't nothing. This money didn't make us, we made the money, we made us. Just get your thoughts together, fam."

"I love you too, my nigga. I know I been off track, but I'ma get behind the wheel and put that shit on cruise control. Listen, fam. I appreciate that pep talk because honestly, I needed that shit and you the one I needed to hear it from," 40 said sincerely.

"A'ight, don't get all emotional and shit and start crying on my soft butter leather seats," Skalez said, joking with his comrade.

"Nigga, fuck you."

"Naw, nigga. Fuck with me."

"You know I do, fam. But for real, Skalez, I've never had a brother or sister, so when we linked up back in the day and grew up together, I started to feel what it was like to have a brother. Now, I just lost one. It took a lot out of me and fucked me up bad," 40 admitted, making eye contact with Skalez.

"You still got another brother left," Skalez reminded him. "But we got to keep moving and succeeding because time don't stop or wait for no man." He gave 40 a pound as he watched him exit the truck.

*** 

Later that night, 40 left his crib to go make a drop out in Hampton on Foxhill to some white guy that had been copping from him. 40 was talking on his cell phone, driving down Mickerson Boulevard.

"Seventeen-Five? Nigga, you crazy! Your ass been listening way too much to Jeezy. Fuck you think you at? Down in Atlanta or Miami somewhere?" Nigga, this Virginia. You lucky I'm charging your ass twenty-four instead of twenty-seven thousand! That's what a nigga around here pushing them for." 40 stopped to hear what the guy had to say before he responded.

The guy mumbled something incoherent that 40 dismissed.

"I thought so. Like maybe your ass was high on this shit or something. But I'll be there in five minutes," 40 said and hung his phone up. *Fuck these niggas think they at? The bottom of the map somewhere.*

As he looked down the street, he saw three cop cars on the side of the road like they were waiting on something. He made a quick right turn on the street right before them.

Turning into an apartment complex, he saw a dumpster with a wooden fence around it. He pulled up to the side of the dumpster, looked around and saw no one.

40 dropped his 45 Ruger in the Timberland bag he had with two bricks of coke, getting out and walking around the little wooden fence near the dumpster.

He looked around the dumpster and tucked the bag inside where he knew it would be when he returned to get it.

*No one should over pack this bitch in 10 minutes,* 40 thought to himself.

He turned back on the street where cops were, feeling better that he didn't have anything on him or in his truck, but something didn't feel right.

*I wouldn't go this way if I didn't have to.*

When he passed the three cop cars, high beams flashed twice on and off.

"What the fuck!" 40 blurted out loud, looking through the rearview mirror and kept going.

When he met the young white dude in the shopping center on Foxhill Road, he parked his Tahoe on the side of West Communications. He saw the white guy getting out his car, heading his way. Then approached his truck and got in.

"What's good, 40?" the guy said.

"This money. That's what's good."

"You got that shit?"

"What kind of question is that? You already know what's up. Where that money at?" He eyed the white dude.

"All forty-eight thousand is in the bag right here for them two kilos of coke."

"Damn, fuck you say it like that for? If I didn't fuck with you, I would think your ass was wearing a wire or some shit." 40 raised a brow.

"Come on, man. What the fuck, dude? You blowing my high. Just gimme the shit so I can be outta here."

"Look, we gotta go back—" was all 40 got out his mouth before the police and unmarked cars came out of nowhere.

The police ran up on his truck with guns pointed at him so fast, he couldn't even utter a word to the white guy.

"What the fuck!"

After that, it was like everything went in slow motion.

\*\*\*

Skalez woke up from the sound of his phone ringing.

"Damn, what time is it?" Paula asked, lying next to him. The clock read 4:30 a.m.

As he picked up the phone, he heard, *"You have a collect call from,* Robert Pulley *at the Hampton City Jail. If you wish to accept and pay for the call—"* Before the automated recording could finish, Skalez pressed 1.

"Man, what the fuck you doing in there? Skalez asked, getting out of bed and walking out of the bedroom.

"It's a long story." 40 sighed.

"Well, I'm listening."

"They got me on some distribution shit, but they didn't catch me with nothing."

"You got bond?"

"Naw, the magistrate denied me and said I'm high risk, so I got to wait until the morning to see a judge."

"Damn, fam. Look, I'ma call Attorney Ashton Wary and tell him to be there in the morning."

"It's damn near 5 o'clock in the morning. How you gon' to do that?" 40 asked.

"Nigga, let me handle this shit, but check it, ain't no need to be breathing through the speaker," Skalez sighed. "So, I'ma see you tomorrow in court, a'ight?"

"A'ight, fam. Good looking out."

"Don't mention it, fam." Skalez got off the phone, shaking his head. *Damn, everything falling apart.*

"What's the matter, baby?" Paula asked, walking down the hallway in her nightgown. Her stomach was poked out from seven months pregnant.

"40 locked up," Skalez said dryly, looking at her.

"For what?"

"You already know, but go back to bed and lay down, baby. I got to call this lawyer for him."

# Chapter 22

The judge wouldn't give 40 a bond and the Feds picked up the case immediately. Only 40's mother and Skalez were in the courtroom the following morning. After court was over, Skalez talked to the attorney for a couple minutes, then left out the building.

"Damn, that Feds shit ain't a good look," Skalez said to himself, knowing the Feds didn't play no games.

A couple weeks had passed and Skalez had been laying around the crib with Paula a lot, just staying away from the streets and staying close to family.

He had been on a straight path since the robbery and murder of Lance. He'd been really trying to stay clear of all the negative situations since the pregnancy. Even though he'd been through some negativity in his life to get where he was today, Skalez was now doing a lot of positive things for himself and others around him.

The streets had taken away all of his loved ones, from his older brother who died at age 30 to Block and recently his cousin to the Feds. Now his last partner, 40, was behind bars. The only family Skalez had left was his mother, Paula, and his unborn baby.

"Damn, I'm the last one standing," he said to out loud, sighing.

Sitting in a chair on the balcony of his master bedroom, Skalez pulled out his blunt of purple haze. As he inhaled the weed, he blew the smoke out through his nostrils slowly, while staring out at the moon, feeling the night breeze hit his body.

"I gotta make it. I'm going to make it," he said lowly to himself.

"Sweetie, when you coming inside? It's getting late. It's almost 11 o'clock," Paula said, sticking her head out the sliding doors of their balcony.

"Gimme a second."

"You alright out here?"

"Yeah, I'ma be in there in a minute, baby."

"Ok," she said and turned to leave.

Skalez cleared his thoughts and smoked his weed before going back inside the house. When he entered the bedroom, he just stopped and looked at Paula, realizing how beautiful she really was and how much he needed her in his life.

"Why you looking at me like that?" Paula asked lying in bed under the covers.

"I'm just admiring your beauty."

"Oh, you still think I'm pretty with this big ole belly?" she said, rubbing her stomach.

As he made his way to the bed, he said, "Our baby girl that's in your stomach only adds to your beauty."

Skalez sat down on the edge of the bed, looking seriously and deeply into Paula eyes.

"Why you staring at me with that look? What's on your mind?"

"What look?"

"That look."

"I'm just taking a peek at your soul and you know what I see?"

"No, what do you see?"

"I see a woman that is not scared to take control when need to be. I see a beautiful woman that wants to raise our child. I see a woman that I desire, need, and want in my life forever," Skalez said, grabbing Paula's hand. "I see a woman I want and would like to walk down the aisle with me." Paula's eyes started to water when she saw him get down on one knee.

"Baby—" she sat up and started to talk, but was cut off.

"Just listen to me, Paula," he whispered. "I see a woman that I want to spend the rest of my life with. I can't see me without you," he said, still on one knee, holding her hand.

"Baby, I love you. So, what it's going to be? Will you marry me?"

"Yes! Yes! Baby, yes! I will marry you," Paula said, crying and pulling Skalez towards her body, slowly kissing him while wrapping her arms and legs around him. "Jermaine, I love you so much, baby."

"I love you too, sweetie." Skalez held her tightly. "Since we met at your school, I knew you were the one for me. I knew I was going to spend the rest of my life with you. You just had that light to you. That ambition you had was sexy. You always went after whatever you wanted," he said, while wiping the tears off her cheeks. "I'm complete now."

"Jermaine, can I just hold you tonight?"

"Baby, I would love for you to do that."

She wrapped her arms around him and they fell asleep together, dreaming of a beautiful future.

# Chapter 23

Lil BJ and Lil Chris sat on the stoop at Lil BJ's mother's house on 36th street smoking a blunt. It had been a month and a half since they laid Block to rest. They'd been on a full-time grind lately. The two of them had been working off a half of kilo for a week, breaking them all the way down to grams and 20-dollar pieces. Lil BJ didn't care about anything. He even hustled off his mother's stoop all times of night. His mother really didn't say anything since he was giving her money daily.

"Lil BJ, you straight?" a friend asked him, walking up to the stoop.

"Yeah. What you want?"

"I want a 20, but I only got 17 dollars."

"Every time your ass come here, your ass got short money. Shit, you about 20 dollars up on me right now."

"Come on, Lil BJ. Don't do me like that."

"Don't do you like what? Shit, don't do me like that. Come on. Let me get that money," Lil BJ said, going in his pocket and pulling out a 20-dollar piece for the fiend.

"Here," he said, throwing it on the ground and walking off.

"I don't know why you acting like you weren't gonna take that bowl head's money," Lil Chris said about the fiend, while passing the blunt.

"Yeah, you know I ain't letting shit go by, but you still gotta do that." As soon as he said that, Lil BJ's older sister walked outside.

"Let me smoke with y'all," Vanessa said, looking at both of them as she sat down.

"Hell naw. Your ass always want to smoke somebody shit up," Lil BJ said.

"What!" Vanessa snapped her head back.

"You heard what I said. What goes around comes around. Now bounce, bitch."

"Fuck you, nigga. You think you something 'cause you getting a couple of dollars," she said, walking past them as she headed down the street.

"You and your sister always going at it," Lil Chris said.

"Man, fuck that bitch. Anyway, I heard that nigga 40 locked up now."

"For what?"

"He caught a coke charge and the Feds got a hold of that shit."

"Damn, we let that nigga slip out. How long he been locked up?"

"At least a month now I heard. We still gonna get the key player, so don't trip." Lil BJ passed the blunt.

"In due time, fam. In due time."

"Aye, you heard about the party Tammy throwing at her house tonight?" Lil BJ asked, spitting on the ground.

"Yeah, Jay told me earlier. Why, you trying to slide through there?"

"Ain't no secret. You know it ain't official unless BJ in it."

"Yeah, I been trying to fuck her for the longest."

"Nigga, she ain't gonna let you hit that shit!"

"Shit, nigga getting paper now. All that shit about to change," Lil Chris said seriously.

"That ain't no lie, but niggas need move up."

"We going to get theirs, fam."

"For real, for real. I'm trying to be so high up, I'm looking down on these niggas like Jesus."

"I feel that. What time is Tammy's party starting?" Lil Chris asked, thinking about her phat ass.

"I think 10 o'clock, but you know we won't show up until 11 or 11:30."

"We gotta go hit the mall and cop an outfit, too."

"No doubt. So, what you waiting on?" Lil BJ said, standing up.

"Well, let's ride out, fam!" Lil Chris said, standing to his feet.

After they left Coliseum Mall out in Hampton with the new outfits they just got, they went out on Shell Road to get some sour Dezil Dro. Riding in Lil Chris's Aura Legend, they pulled over in front of a blue house on Kentucky Avenue off Shell Road.

"Hold on. I'll be right back," Lil BJ said and got out the car, walking to the house.

While Lil Chris sat waiting, he started texting one of his little girlfriends.

"Damn, what the fuck that nigga doing in there?' he said after five minutes.

As soon as he did, Lil BJ was walking out the door.

'Bout time, Lil Chris said to himself.

"Yo, that nigga Dalonty's sister is fat as shit," Lil BJ said, getting into the car.

"Fuck that bitch, fam. How much smoke you get? "Lil Chris asked, pulling off.

"I got an ounce of that sour. You know you paying for half this shit, too, nigga."

"I already know. We gotta hurry up and get one of them pipe heads to go. I ain't going in no ABC store. You know a nigga can't go up in the party empty handed."

As they pulled up at the house party at 12 o'clock, they parked five houses down because it was packed. It was people standing around outside in the front and some in were the street. Getting out of Lil Chris's Acura, smoke was coming from the car as they opened the doors. Walking to the house, they each had two bottles of Remy XO in both hands.

"Damn, look at shorty right there with the red skirt on?" Lil Chris pointed with the bottle in his hand.

"Yeah, she fatter then a mu'fucker. I bet I fuck something tonight."

Walking up to the house, they heard music all the way outside. As they walked inside the two-story house, people that knew them, spoke as they walked through the crowd.

"Hey, BJ," one of the young cuties said as they passed.

Walking into the kitchen, they dropped a bottle apiece off at the table where the alcohol was at, keeping a bottle each for themselves.

As they made their way to the living room where all the action was, Lil Chris saw Tammy standing by the stairs looking like she was playing the hostess.

"There goes Tammy right there," Lil Chris said. "Damn, she looking good."

"Yeah, she a'ight," Lil BJ responded, looking over at Tammy.

"I'm about to go holla at her." Lil Chris licked his lips.

"Go ahead. I'm going over here where the shorties at," Lil BJ said, walking into the huge living while Lil Chris went to go holla at Tammy.

Making his way to the living room was like walking into a soldout concert. Everybody was bumping into each other. Lil BJ was stealing feels on the girls as they passed them, grabbing their asses and keeping it moving. People were dancing everywhere. They were in the hallways and on the stairs. There were people everywhere.

Looking from the center of the living room floor, Lil BJ saw two girls dancing, kissing, and grinding all over each other.

"Gotta to drink to that," he said, popping the top on the bottle of the Remy.

As he took a swig of the liquor, a girl just came in front of him and started grinding and dancing on him.

"Damn, what's up, little momma?" Lil BJ said, but the girl didn't say anything. She just looked at him seductively and turned around, throwing her ass on him.

While she was popping her ass on him, he just started doing a two-step, holding his bottle in his right hand with his left hand grabbing her waist. When the house DJ switched Ludacris' "Pussy Popping" to reggae, the girl started winding her hips like a snake and grinding her ass on him. Her skirt started to rise and her thong started to show.

As Lil BJ felt her ass and thong grinding all on his dick, he looked down and saw her ass working him. His dick got rock hard. She turned her head, looked at him and started to smile, reaching back and grabbing a handful of Lil BJ's dick.

"Nice," she said and kept working her hips like a snake on him. The next thing they heard was somebody shooting.

*Pop, Pop, Pop, Pop!*

As Lil BJ dropped his bottle and ducked, his natural reflexes kicked in as he grabbed the 38 Snubnose out of his back pocket.

"Damn, it's dark in here. I gotta find Lil Chris," Lil BJ said, hearing the shots that made everyone stop and scatter around. Even Lil BJ, who was moving with the crowd.

When he went into the hallway to get out the house, he saw a guy lying on the ground with Tammy kneeling down by his side.

"Where the fuck is Lil Chris at?" Lil BJ asked himself.

"Lil BJ! Come on, nigga. Hurry the fuck up!" Lil Chris said, yelling to him from down the street.

Lil BJ heard him and started running towards the car. When he hopped in, Lil Chris sped off.

"Man, what the fuck happened back there?" Lil BJ asked.

"Fam, I had to let a couple off in the nigga,"

"You what? That was you?"

"Yeah, that nigga tried to stunt and shit. Popping all fly out the mouth in front of shorty. Talking about that's his girl and shit and I better back the fuck up and all that shit. I was gonna let the nigga make it until he put his hands on me," he explained as they turned down Madison Avenue.

"Damn, fam. We weren't even in that bitch thirty minutes, but it's better him than you."

"You better believe it!" Lil Chris said.

"Man, I had this bad little bitch on me, too."

"I hope nobody mention my name, fam, to the police or nothing."

"No bullshit," Lil BJ said, taking a peek through the side mirror on the car.

"I ain't even going to go to the crib tonight."

"What, you trying to come and lay low at my spot?"

"Naw, I'ma go head to Cassie's house out in Hampton."

"Shit, you don't need to be in this car for real, for real."

"I know, fam."

"That nigga was looking fucked up when I saw him before I came out the house," Lil BJ said.

"Fuck that nigga. He put his hands on the wrong nigga. I hope I offed that nigga, for real."

"I hope so, too, 'cause we don't have no time for a nigga trying to sneak a nigga," Lil BJ said, checking his side mirror again.

When Lil Chris dropped him off, he headed out to Hampton to one of the girl's crib. He called to let her know he was on his way and to leave the door unlocked. While driving, he thought about the second body he just caught in the last month in a half and didn't feel any remorse about it.

# Chapter 24

While sitting in Portsmouth City Jail, 40 had a lot of time to think, recapping every step he took that landed him in his situation. During his stay in Bedrock, as they called the jail, he came across a female deputy that worked there. They'd been dealing with each other for the last couple of weeks. And in just two weeks, she'd bought him a cell phone and some weed. 40 still had connects out there in the streets and people that still hustled for him, so it wasn't nothing for him to give her a few dollars. But the crazy thing was her coming and pushing up on him.

After she took him one night from the first floor to the nurse's station, he fucked her and it had been on ever since.

"Robert Pulley, get ready to go the nurse," a male deputy yelled into the cell block.

"A'ight, give a second," 40 replied.

40 knew that was Lisa, the female deputy, working to get him down there. After brushing his teeth and freshening up, he made his way to the door of the cellblock to be let out.

As he walked down the hallway to get on the elevator, he got stares from the other inmates. Some knew who he was and where he was from, but Portsmouth dudes didn't fuck with Newport News dudes and vice-versa.

40, however, wasn't on no geographical shit. He figured if you were a good individual, he could get some money with you. Fuck where you are from. It was about where them dollars came from.

As he made it to the nurse's station, the male officer left, leaving him alone with the nurse. As soon as the nurse shut the door, she said, "Lisa will be on her way down. She's coming from the second floor."

The good thing about the nurse's office was there were no cameras. The nurse and Lisa had been best friends ever since middle school, so it was always easy for them to scheme to get him down on there for some one on one time.

"So, what's up with your boy, Skalez?" the nurse asked with a smile.

"I told you my man married, but I got my fam Raymond for you."

"How does he look?"

"I ain't gon' to get into all of that. You can see for yourself. Write his number down." After he gave her the number and they talked for a couple of minutes, Lisa walked in.

"Hey, sexy," Lisa said to 40.

"What's good, shorty?" 40 replied, sitting on the examination table.

"Well, I'ma be right outside, so y'all hurry up this time," the nurse said and walked out.

As soon as the door closed, they went straight at it like a boxing match, knowing they had to get it over with quickly. When she knelt down, she unbuttoned his orange jumper by the crotch area and took out his dick.

As she started bobbing her head back and forth, he grabbed the back of her head and started fucking her mouth like it was a pussy.

"Fuck! Ahhh," he said, starting to moan.

He felt himself about to cum after a few minutes, but stopped her and pulled her up. As he quickly unbuttoned her belt with all the keys and mace on it, she took off the walkie-talkie and placed it on the examination tale. She then bent over and grabbed her ankles, allowing him to slide his dick inside her.

"Damn, baby. You feel good," 40 said as he entered her.

While he was pumping and pounding from the back, she was moaning, letting out small screams. As he was looking down on her red ass, he spread both cheeks from the bottom and started grinding into her viciously.

"Uh, uh, uh. Cum in me, baby. Don't pull out. Let me feel your hot nut in me," she moaned.

40 couldn't control himself, cumming all in her. "Aghhhhh," 40 let out.

While they fixed themselves up, 40 looked at her as she got herself together.

*Damn it's something about a female in a uniform,* he thought to himself.

"Here," she said, taking out an ounce of weed out her bra and passing it to him.

"No doubt," he said, stuffing it down his boxer briefs.

As they exited the office, they both spoke to the nurse and kept it pushing. Lisa took him back to his cellblock and told him to call her when she got off at six.

As he went back on the block, he went to his cell and tied a sheet around the bars so no one could see inside. He didn't have to worry about anyone because he didn't have a celly.

Sitting on his bunk, he reached in his boxer briefs and pulled out the weed, placing it inside his mattress.

*I'ma smoke this shit later.*

40 didn't need any money, but he gave some to a guy named Bear from Norfolk that was on the block with him so he could make a few dollars.

He took a liking to the dude as soon as they started kicking it, but not enough to tell him about the cellphone and a C.O. bitch he was fucking.

After he put the weed up, he got on his knees, reached under the bed and removed the little brick that was connected to the wall. The hole was only big enough to put his hand in. After he grabbed the cellphone, he got back on his bunk and started dialing numbers, listening to it ring on the other end.

"Hello," the guy, said answering the phone.

"Good looking out on that Timberland," 40 said, talking about the weed.

"Oh yeah? Anything for you, fam."

"Everything looking good out there on the ballcourt?"

"So, so. We got an injured player."

"Damn, who is it?" 40 asked with concern in his voice.

"Dre Jack."

"He all right?"

"Naw, he was taken out of the game for good."

40 sighed, thinking how shit was starting to get worse by the week. *Damn, I gotta get out of here.*

His lieutenant Jay was holding shit down for him in his absence, but it was like the longer he was away, the more shit happened.

"Who y'all playing?" 40 said.

"Some nobodies," Jay said, telling him that they didn't know who did Dre Jack in.

"Aye look, I'ma get off this phone for now, but y'all gotta have more defense, fam. This sport we play is for keeps. And find out who those team players were and their coach. And don't play with 'em. Just end the game!"

40 hung up the phone upset. "Damn, one of my block huggers got hit," he said to himself. After placing the cellphone back, he sat on his bunk thinking about how he needed a smoke.

"Yo, Bear?" 40 yelled out.

"Yeah."

"Come here real quick."

When Bear entered the cell, he sat on the sink with his foot on the toilet that was connected to it.

"You trying to smoke?" 40 asked, reaching into the cut in his mattress and pulling out the weed.

"What type of question is that? You know a nigga like me trying to smoke," Bear replied.

As 40 gave Bear some weed to roll up, he took half an ounce and put it in an envelope.

"This for you. Just bring me back half of what you make, a'ight?"

"That's what's up. You know a nigga can use that. Hey, where the batteries and razor at?"

"Here." 40 grabbed the utensil from the corner of the bed to light the weed.

"You know these niggas in here mad cause you getting weed in here, right?"

"I don't give a fuck! Fuck these niggas," 40 said all loud, hoping that one tier of the ear hustlers would hear him outside his cell.

"Man, you wild. That's why I fuck with you and because you a real nigga."

"You in your early twenties and carry yourself like you in your mid-thirties. These niggas just mad that you from across the water out of Bad News, but over in Portsmouth in their jail getting money. Fuck these niggas and this jail. I ain't asked to be in this bitch. They mad because a nigga getting some funky ass commissary. That shit ain't no money," 40 said, pointing at three laundry bags full of food.

Bear looked at the bags of food 40 was talking about.

"That shit ain't nothing to a nigga like me, bad body broke ass niggas," he said. He grabbed the three bags and dragged them to the day room where everybody was, dumping all the items on the floor.

"Y'all can have that shit. That shit ain't nothing. I'm from East End Bad News and if a nigga in here got a problem with me, come holla at me," 40 said, talking loud as the guys in the day room just looked at him not saying anything. "Just as I thought!" 40 said, turning around and walking back to his cell with Bear right behind him.

"What the fuck you do that for? You could've just gave that shit to me," Bear told him, looking at 40 like he lost his mind.

"Fam, that shit ain't nothing. I fuck with you, so you eat when I eat and that's every second of the day. So fuck them niggas and let's smoke."

# Chapter 25

Skalez drove through the city, contemplating his next venture. He wanted to be part owner of The Exclusive Wheels car dealership off on Jefferson Avenue. The owner of the dealership just had made him an offer. Skalez knew the guy was in debt and needed the cash to keep the business going. As he drove past Fresh to Death barbershop, he saw the light on in the shop and his cousin Raymond's car was parked out front.

*Damn it's nine o'clock at night. What that nigga still doing at my shop,* Skalez thought to himself. He made a u-turn and parked across the street, getting out of the car and walking to the front door of the shop.

He pulled the door to open it, but it was locked, so he went through his keys on his key chain and put the key into the shop door. As he opened the door, he went in and looked around, noticing there was no one in the front.

Shutting the door and walking to the back where the office was, he saw the door was open. He stood there, peeking through the crack of the door and he couldn't believe what he saw. He took the 45 Ruger off his hip and pushed the door open.

"What the fuck!" Raymond said caught in the act, standing on a chair looking back at Skalez in shock. Raymond had been hiding coke in the vent in the office for the past couple of weeks.

"Aye look, Skalez. I was scared to put it somewhere else—" Raymond started to explain, stepping down from the chair before Skalez cut him off.

"Shut the fuck up! Didn't I tell you if I catch you doing some shit like this what I was going to do?" Skalez spat, cocking the gun back, putting one in the chamber.

"My fault, cousin. I can take it out right now." Raymond was *shook*.

"Cousin, my ass. If you wanted to play the family role, you would've followed the family rules. You trying to fuck with my money, my family and with me."

"I would never do that," Raymond told him, stretching out his arms.

"Fuck you mean? What happens if the police would have ran up in here and found that shit? Who you think they gonna grab for that shit? What, you would have took the charge for me or something, huh?"

"Yeah, I would have taken them for you, Skalez."

"Nigga, stop faking. You wouldn't have took shit."

"Come on, fam. I'm sorry."

"Don't fam me. Fam wouldn't have tried to jeopardize me and my place of business," Skalez said, shaking his head. "Talking about you would've took the charges. Hmph, you know what? Take these."

*Bong, bong, bong!* was all that was heard as Skalez fired three shots off in his chest.

"Dumb ass nigga. I told your ass. Now look at you," Skalez yelled, looking down at his dead cousin.

"Fuck, look at what you made me do. Now I gotta clean all this shit up."

Putting his gun back on his waist, he started going through Raymond's pockets and got his keys. Walking back to the front of the barbershop, he went to Raymond's Expedition.

Hopping in his truck, he started it up and drove it to the back of the shop. Getting out of the truck in the back alley, he looked around and saw no one. Unlocking the back door and walking to his office, he stopped and looked at the corpse.

*Damn, it wasn't suppose to be like this. Now, need something to roll this nigga up in.*

He went out the office and opened the closet door next to the bathroom. When he opened it, it he saw nothing but towels until he looked down and saw some blankets.

Grabbing three blankets, he went back in the office and laid it out beside Raymond's dead body. It wasn't a lot of blood, just a puddle. As he rolled the body over onto the blanket, he wrapped him all the way up.

Dragging the body to the backdoor by its feet, he stopped before he opened it. Then he looked both ways as he walked out the back of the shop. Not seeing anyone, he walked over to Raymond's truck and opened the back door.

Walking back, he started pulling the corpse towards the truck. After he got Raymond's dead body in the back seat, he shut the door, hopped in the driver's seat and peeled off.

*Fuck it. I'ma take this crab nigga down to the docks.*

As he drove through the streets of downtown Newport News at 10 o'clock at night with a body in the back seat, Skalez was paranoid. He knew the cops would pull you over for anything.

As he made it down to 6th street by the waterfront and the boats, he pulled up along side a little cliff. Getting out the truck, he walked over to the cliff and looked down in the water.

"Yeah, this nigga about to go swimming," he said, walking back to the truck and opening the back door. As he reached for his feet, he heard something. Turning around quicly, he saw a cat running by the truck.

*Man, let me hurry up and get the fuck outta here.*

When Skalez pulled the corpse out of the truck, its head made a noise, hitting the footsteps of the truck. Just being reckless, he took him to the cliff and rolled him into the water.

He looked at his older cousin, sinking to the bottom of the water. Sighing, Skalez looked up at the full moon and took a deep breath.

Making his way back to the barbershop in Raymond's Expedition, he thought about setting the truck on fire.

"Yeah, that's what I'm going to do after I clean up the shop. Take it somewhere and put some flames to it, then catch a cab back and get my truck." He coached himself.

After cleaning the mess up at the shop, he took Raymond's truck across town to 26th street and set it on fire.

Skalez walked a few blocks away and hopped in a cab that had been waiting for him.

Heading back to the shop, his cell phone rung. He looked at the phone, not recognizing the number.

"Who this?" Skalez answered as he sat in the back of the cab.

"What's good, fam?"

"Oh shit. What's good, my nigga?" He recognized 40's voice.

"Ain't nothing. Just checking in with you."

"Fo' sho'. It's kinda late for phone calls," Skalez said, looking out the cab back seat window, heading back to the shop.

"Yeah, you know I get around. These fuckers can't keep me down long. I gotta let my mind travel some kind a way. And this right here is a good way, but what's good with you?" asked 40.

Skalez sighed and said, "Too much, fam. Just thinking about what just took place."

"Yeah?"

"It's like family ain't family no more. You try to look out for people, but it's like the more you try, the more they try to take you down. I ain't going down, fam. So, I eliminated the problem before it started to get out of hand. You feel me?"

"Yeah, I understand clearly," 40 said, knowing that Skalez had to put in some work. "You gotta do what you gotta do. You can't let anybody interfere with yours."

Pulling up a block away from the barbershop, he paid the cab fare and got out. Still talking to 40 and walking, he saw a black-tinted out, Acura Legend cruising by him slowly. Eyeing the car and turning his head when it passed him, he said, "What the fuck them niggas creeping all slow for?"

"Who you talking about?" 40 asked.

"I don't know who them clowns was, but yeah, I might fuck with dude on the car lot to add to the piggy bank," Skalez replied, getting into his QX56 and driving off.

"That's a good look. Real good."

"Hey, you got that money I sent you, right?"

"Yeah, I got the receipt yesterday. Good looking out, but you know a nigga ain't needing or wanting for nothing, right? You don't have to keep sending me money every week. I'm straight."

"Nigga, you fam. I don't care how straight your ass is. I'm just making sure your ass is super straight." 40 started laughing, but not too loud that the others could hear.

"I can't wait to bust through these doors."

"Me neither. Nigga, I need you out here. I miss you, fam."

"I'ma do a lot of shit different this time around. I gotta beat this case."

"It's all gonna come through, believe that. Just believe what I say when I tell you. It's all gonna come together."

"Hey, no doubt, fam. Let me get off this phone," 40 said quickly, disconnecting the call.

Skalez placed the cell phone in his lap as he turned on Chestnut Avenue, heading to Mercury Boulevard. He was lost in his thoughts about of him killing his cousin.

He drove a little further, thinking about his aunt, mother, sister and Raymond's sisters who would take his disappearance hard.

He thought back on how his mother took his older brother's death and it wasn't good. He had to do what he had to do before it got out of hand, but his cousin he went against his word. His phone started to ring again, breaking him out of his thoughts.

"I'm on my way," he said, already knowing it was Paula calling.

"All right, I was just wondering where you were," she said.

"How's my baby doing?"

"She just was moving around."

"Oh yeah? She might be wondering why she haven't felt my hand over your belly."

"Yeah, probably so."

"I'm 10 minutes away, all right?" Skalez told her.

"Ok, sweetie. I'll see you when you get home."

"Alright, baby," he said and hung up the phone.

# Chapter 26

Three months had past and things still hadn't changed for the good and some for the worse. Skalez and Paula had a beautiful baby girl, weighing 8 pounds and 2 ounces and 21 inches long. They named her Akeemah. 40 was still in jail, waiting for trial with his Fed beef.

Sitting in Portsmouth City Jail, where they held federal inmates, was a major headache. Everything was fucked up. The food was garbage and there were cockroaches and mice everywhere. There were dudes getting sliced up everyday by each other. They had no AC, so they had little fans placed in every cellblock.

Fights were random and it was hot in there, so that was a reason enough. 40 kept commissaries and he always looked out for the unfortunate that didn't have anything. Skalez made sure that he was straight even though 40 had his own cash.

*"You have a collect call from—"* Skalez pressed 1, accepting the call before the recording could finish.

"What's good, my nigga?" Skalez said.

"Ain't shit. Just thinking about the big day next week," 40 replied.

"Yeah, I know. Me too."

"You know I was reading the paper today and it said Adam James was found dead at his crib," 40 said with a little excitement.

"Yeah?" Skalez said like he was shocked at the news, but already knew the informant's head had been push back to the white meat.

"I talked to my lawyer today and he said the only thing they have now is the tape they got me on when he was wired, but that's not much of nothing."

"That's good because a nigga need you home, fam," Skalez said.

"No doubt! Congratulations on the engagement and baby, too."

"You told me that already," Skalez said, laughing at his friend.

"I know, but I just want to know that I am proud of you. You grew and came a long way and learned to settle for what you already have."

"I appreciate that. You know I need my best man here at home."

*"You have 1 minute,"* the operator said.

"I love you, fam. Take it slow in there and I'll see you at home next week."

"A'ight, fam," Skalez said and disconnected the call. *Damn it's six o'clock already,* Skalez said to himself, looking at his Rolex watch.

*** 

After he laid his sleeping daughter, Akeemah, down, he walked out her room and went down stairs.

When he entered the kitchen, he walked up to Paula while she was washing dishes and wrapped his arms around her waist.

"Oh shit, boy," she said, dropping the plate in the water, turning her head at him. "You scared the shit out of me."

"That used to be my job," Skalez said, while standing behind her, hugging her.

"Yeah, I know. I'm glad you switched professions."

"Yeah, a lot of people are, too," Skalez replied, kissing her on the cheek, then releasing her. "Baby, I gotta pick the money up from the shops real quick. You need something while I'm gone?"

"Uh, no. I'm alright. Oh yeah, some pampers."

"Damn, little momma ran through both of them boxes already?"

"You know she shits a lot."

"Don't be talking about my little girl like that," Skalez told her, playing.

"Or what?" Paula challenged him, walking up on Skalez.

"Nothing, if you keep looking at me like that." Skalez threw his hands in the air surrendering. "But look, let me get outta here before we start something." Quickly kissing Paula, he squeezed her ass.

"Ohhhh!"

"Just be ready when I get back," he said, walking off.

*** 

Reaching the shop, he wasted no time getting the money so he could get back to Paula and put it on her. It's like ever since Paula had the baby, she'd been extra horny and the sex had been crazy lately. Skalez went in and out the beauty salon, collecting the money from his mother.

Walking out the beauty and nail salon, he went next door to the barbershop. It felt different every time he went there because Raymond was no longer managing the place.

He had replaced Raymond with Torell who'd been working there since the place opened. People still didn't know what had happened to Raymond. People thought he either ran off with his connect's work or that the connect may have killed him for shortening him on some money because Raymond was known to betray a nigga and play with his money. But only Skalez knew what really happened.

After collecting his money, Skalez went outside and walked across the street to his Infinite QX56. While driving to Food Lion to get Akeemah some pampers, he was lost in his thoughts.

*I'm glad I didn't take that ole nigga Charley up on his deal with the car lot.*

The Feds ran into the car dealership for selling hot cars.

"I'm going to just keep doing what I do," Skalez said out loud.

Pulling up in the garage of his house, he got out the truck, got the boxes of pampers and shut the door. Going into the house it was dark, so he flicked the hallway lights on with his index finger, still holding the box.

When he sat the box of pampers down by the stairs, he went into the kitchen for something to drink. As he was got a glass out the cabinet, he noticed a note on the counter. He picked it up and started to read it.

*By the time you start reading this letter, I will be enjoying myself upstairs, waiting for you to accompany me. Are you still down there reading this? Come on upstairs. I got something to show you.*

Skalez smiled slyly, laid the note back on the counter, and then went upstairs.

When he got to the door and opened it, he saw Paula butt ass naked. She was lying on the bed with her legs opened, playing with her clit while caressing her breast with the other hand.

It was dark in the room, but the candles she had lit around the bed had a nice dim light to it. As he looked at her playing with herself, his dick got hard immediately. He started to undress and got closer to the bed.

When he reached the foot of the bed, she told him to stop right there. As he complied, she took her fingers out her pussy and tasted her juices. Then got on all fours and started to crawl to him. Cat Woman didn't have nothing on this crawl.

She stopped when she reached the peak of his dick. Still on her knees and hands, she started to lick the tip of his dick. She took more of him in her mouth, pulling on it with just her jaws with no hands. He let her do her thing without putting his hands on her head.

"Ahhh. Damn, baby."

"Lay on your back, baby," Paula said, coming off his dick. When he lay on his back, she stood over him and slid down, doing a split slowly while spreading her pussy lips. "Got damn," Skalez said, watching her. As she came down on his dick, he entered her and Paula eyes closed.

"Oh my God, Jermaine." She started bouncing up and down on his manhood slowly, still in the split position. He reached around her, grabbing her right ass cheek, pulling her ass and pussy lips apart. "Ohhh," Paula moaned, then he started to pump harder. The more he pumped, the more she couldn't stand it. So she got out of the position and just straddled him. "Jermaine, I love you so much, baby." She leaned down to kiss him.

"I love you too, baby."

"Ahhh, damn. I feel it coming already." She sat on him and started to rock her hips back and forth instead of up and down.

"I'm about to cum, too." He grabbed both of her ass cheeks, breathing heavily.

"Uhhh, uh. I'm cum—cumming. Cum with me, baby," Paula said, moaning louder. "You feel it?" she asked before she released all over Skalez's dick.

Skalez couldn't hold it any longer before he exploded inside her. "Ahhhhh, baby! Ahhhhh!" Skalez grunted, lying on top of Paula, trying to get his breath.

They broke out of their sex trance when they heard Akeemah crying over the speaker of the baby monitor.

"Shit," Skalez said.

## Chapter 27

40 and Skalez talked on the phone as he prepared for his court hearing that determined if he would go free or not. "Tomorrow is the big day, fam," said 40.

"I know. I'm gonna be there, bright and early," Skalez replied, driving in his Infinite truck.

"This shit got my nerves bad for real. I swear I grew about six grey hairs in this bitch."

"Shit, that's how it is when you facing 35 years, but you good, homie. You about to walk and be back on this side of the wall."

"Yeah, I know. I just—Man, fuck all that. What you about to do?" 40 said, changing the subject as he tried not to think about his court situation.

"Fam, you crazy, but I just dropped some money off to Ms. Johnson."

"Oh word? How Block's Mom Dukes doing?"

"She's holding up. She asked about you and told me to tell you that you are in her prayers."

"That's what's up because I need all the prayer I can get."

"Hey, whatever happened to that snow bunny that Block used to fuck with?"

"You talking about Christy?"

"Yeah, her."

"Fam, that bitch is on it for real. She coked up like a mu'fucker."

"Damn, I never thought shorty got down like that," 40 said.

"Niggas saying that bitch look like a zombie and shit. Shorty might be on that yay for real," Skalez replied, checking his mirrors as he drove.

"She must've took Block's death hard as shit."

"You have one minute," the recording said.

"I hate hearing that shit." 40 cussed the automated recording. "I'ma see you in the morning, fam."

"A'ight, fam, Just breathe easy. It'll be all good tomorrow," Skalez said, reassuring his man that things was going to be alright.

"No doubt."

"A'ight," Skalez said, disconnecting the call.

As soon as Skalez hung up the phone, it started ringing again. Looking at the caller ID, he knew it was Paula.

"What's up, baby?"

"I just wanted to let you know me and little momma are on our way to my mother's house," Paula said.

"A'ight, just call me when you get there."

"Okay baby, I love you."

"Love you, too," Skalez replied and waited for her to hang up.

Pulling up to the little waterfront on Chesapeake Bay Avenue, he parked his truck and started to look at water as the sun began to set. This was one his favorite spots he would go to to gather his thoughts.

Taking a deep breath and slowly exhaling, he said, to himself, "Damn, I remember when I didn't have a pot to piss in and now I got a business and became a family man. It's crazy how things and situations can change a lot. You got choices, chances and changes you got to go through in life. You got to make a choice and take a chance to make a change whatever it may be. It all starts with a choice. Be risk taker. They say when you try hard, you die hard."

*Well, I guess I'ma die hard because I'm damn sure a risk taker. I stopped trying and started doing,* Skalez thought. As his mind drifted to his mother, he knew she'd been through a lot as a single mom and did everything she could've done to provide for her two sons.

When he was young, he didn't understand all the circumstances and sacrifices she had to go through just to make sure they were all right. But as he got older, he showed more appreciation and love towards her every day.

Every day was Mother's Day for Momma Mona. Even if he just called to tell her he loved her, he stayed showing her and Paula love with flowers at least twice out the week.

Twenty minutes had passed when he started up the truck and left the waterfront.

Making his way to his home he thought, *I hope that nigga beat this case because I damn sure can't lose another brother to these streets.*

Riding to the crib, he had the music off, just thinking about everything. Pulling up in the driveway and parking he thought, *Damn, she didn't even leave the porch light on when she left.*

Getting out of the truck, he shut the door and walked off, hitting the button on his key to lock the doors to his truck.

Reaching the front door to his house, he put the key in and unlocked the door, opening it. As soon as he took the first step in the house, he was struck with the butt of a pistol on the side of the jaw.

"Argh!" he yelled, falling to the floor from the unexpected blow. The guy that hit him with the gun shut the door, while the masked gunmen stood over him.

"Where the fuck the money at?" the tall one asked.

"What? Nigga, I ain't got no money. Fuck y'all," Skalez said angrily, rubbing his chin as he laid on the floor.

"Oh yeah? You a tough guy, huh?" the tall guy said and started smacking Skalez in the side of the face with his gun.

"You wanna be tough, huh?"

*Whop! Whop!*

The gut kept smacking him with the pistol. *Damn, this is how it's going to go,* Skalez thought after the guy stopped pounding him.

"I got something for your ass," Skalez said lowly.

"What you say?" the tall guy snapped.

"I said I got something for you."

The other guy just stood there with a gun in his hand, just looking on quietly. Skalez realized they didn't even search him to see if he had a gun on him. *Amateurs,* he thought.

They didn't know what they were doing or getting into. As Skalez got up, the tall guy said with the gun pointed it at his head and said, "Lead the way."

Skalez gave him a look that could kill and started to walk. Skalez noticed the guy had a little limp with his walk. When they reached his daughter Akeemah's room, he went to the closet.

"Don't do anything stupid," the tall guy warned him, doing all the talking. Skalez knelt down and started turning the knob on the small safe in the walk-in closet.

*Damn, this shit feel so familiar,* Skalez thought. He cut his eyes to see if they were watching and sure enough, they were watching with hawk eyes. When the safe opened, the tall guy got him to pass the money back. *Second mistake,* Skalez thought.

"A'ight," Skalez said. Before passing the money back, he saw the tall guy put his gun in his waist and peeped at the other guy just standing there on post with his gun at his side. *Amateur ass nigga. I got something for their ass, alright,* Skalez thought to himself.

After he passed a couple of stacks back, he reached back in the safe and grabbed a stack of money with his left hand and passed it back. Then he reached in the safe with his right hand and grabbed his Glock 19.

With no safety on, he put one in the head, then hit him with two slugs to his chest quickly. As the guy fell down, he pointed the gun at the other guy, but it was too late as Skalez took a bullet to the shoulder.

The guy ran over and kicked the gun from beside him as Skalez hit the floor. When Skalez looked up at the masked man, he stared at him for the first time.

"You remember when you said everybody got a position to play and everybody don't get paid the same? It's like you're on a NBA team!"

"What the fuck you talking about?" Skalez said, not knowing what he was getting at.

As the guy took off his mask, Skalez screwed his face up like he ate something sour. "You bitch ass nigga," Skalez said, looking up at Lil BJ, fucked up that he would do something like this.

"That's the same shit Block said before we killed him. And you were right. I was on the bench and I been watching you play the whole time, sitting side court on the other side," Lil BJ said with his gun, pointing down at Skalez.

"And two of your most valuable players are out of the game. One of them was terminated and the other one fouled out. It's the fourth quarter and you down by two, but the time ran and the buzzer has sounded off."

*Just when I got my life in order,* Skalez thought to himself.

"You know there comes a time in a person's life where you're just fed up and you have no choice. It may be for the good or even for the worse, and sometimes you may do some bad things, but end up turning it into something positive. But one thing I do know, it's always someone out there that will try to take what you got just to get where you're at. So, guard what you have with your life because it could be easily taken away."

"Nigga, fuck you!" Skalez barked before the bullets riddled his body and he embraced his death.

*Bock, Bock, Bock, Bock!*

Lil BJ kept squeezing the trigger until the whole clip was empty.

"Naw, nigga, fuck you," Lil BJ said, grabbing the bag of money and walking out the room.

He left Skalez' house feeling invincible, but little did he know things weren't a sweet as they seemed. Because the very next day, Robert Pulley A.K.A 40 was found not guilty and was released from jail.

Now, shit was about to get serious!


*To Be Continued...*
When the Streets Clap Back 2
Coming Soon

## Coming Soon from Lock Down Publications/Ca$h Presents

BOW DOWN TO MY GANGSTA

By **Ca$h**

TORN BETWEEN TWO

By **Coffee**

BLOOD STAINS OF A SHOTTA **II**

By **Jamaica**

WHEN THE STREETS CLAP BACK **II**

By **Jibril Williams**

STEADY MOBBIN

By **Marcellus Allen**

BLOOD OF A BOSS **V**

By **Askari**

BRIDE OF A HUSTLA **III**

By **Destiny Skai**

WHEN A GOOD GIRL GOES BAD **II**

By **Adrienne**

LOVE & CHASIN' PAPER **II**

By **Qay Crockett**

THE HEART OF A GANGSTA **III**

By **Jerry Jackson**

LOYAL TO THE GAME **IV**

By **T.J. & Jelissa**

A DOPEBOY'S PRAYER **II**

By **Eddie "Wolf" Lee**

IF LOVING YOU IS WRONG… **III**

By **Jelissa**

BLOODY COMMAS **III**

SKI MASK CARTEL

By **T.J. Edwards**

BLAST FOR ME **II**

By **Ghost**

A DISTINGUISHED THUG STOLE MY HEART **III**

By **Meesha**

ADDICTIED TO THE DRAMA **II**

By **Jamila Mathis**

LIPSTICK KILLAH

By **Mimi**

**Available Now**

RESTRAINING ORDER **I & II**

By **CA$H & Coffee**

LOVE KNOWS NO BOUNDARIES **I II & III**

By **Coffee**

RAISED AS A GOON I, II & III

By **Ghost**

LAY IT DOWN **I & II**

LAST OF A DYING BREED

By **Jamaica**

LOYAL TO THE GAME

LOYAL TO THE GAME II

LOYAL TO THE GAME III

By **TJ & Jelissa**

BLOODY COMMAS I & II

By **T.J. Edwards**

IF LOVING HIM IS WRONG…I & II

By **Jelissa**

A DISTINGUISHED THUG STOLE MY HEART I & II

By **Meesha**

PUSH IT TO THE LIMIT

By **Bre' Hayes**

BLOOD OF A BOSS **I, II, III & IV**

By **Askari**

THE STREETS BLEED MURDER **I, II & III**

THE HEART OF A GANGSTA I & II

By **Jerry Jackson**

CUM FOR ME

CUM FOR ME 2

CUM FOR ME 3

An **LDP Erotica Collaboration**

BRIDE OF A HUSTLA **I & II**

THE FETTI GIRLS **I, II& III**

By **Destiny Skai**

WHEN A GOOD GIRL GOES BAD

By **Adrienne**

A GANGSTER'S REVENGE **I II III & IV**

THE BOSS MAN'S DAUGHTERS

THE BOSS MAN'S DAUGHTERS II

A SAVAGE LOVE **I & II**

BAE BELONGS TO ME

A HUSTLER'S DECEIT I, II

By **Aryanna**

A KINGPIN'S AMBITON

A KINGPIN'S AMBITION **II**

I MURDER FOR THE DOUGH

By **Ambitious**

TRUE SAVAGE

TRUE SAVAGE II

TRUE SAVAGE **III**

By **Chris Green**

A DOPEBOY'S PRAYER

By **Eddie "Wolf" Lee**

WHAT ABOUT US **I & II**

NEVER LOVE AGAIN

THUG ADDICTION

By **Kim Kaye**

THE KING CARTEL **I, II & III**

By **Frank Gresham**

THESE NIGGAS AIN'T LOYAL **I, II & III**

By **Nikki Tee**

GANGSTA SHYT **I II &III**

By **CATO**

THE ULTIMATE BETRAYAL

By **Phoenix**

BOSS'N UP **I , II & III**

By **Royal Nicole**

I LOVE YOU TO DEATH

**By Destiny J**

I RIDE FOR MY HITTA

I STILL RIDE FOR MY HITTA

By **Misty Holt**

LOVE & CHASIN' PAPER

By **Qay Crockett**

TO DIE IN VAIN

By **ASAD**

BROOKLYN HUSTLAZ

By **Boogsy Morina**

BROOKLYN ON LOCK I & II

By **Sonovia**

GANGSTA CITY

By **Teddy Duke**

## **BOOKS BY LDP'S CEO, CA$H**

TRUST IN NO MAN

TRUST IN NO MAN 2

TRUST IN NO MAN 3

BONDED BY BLOOD

SHORTY GOT A THUG

THUGS CRY

THUGS CRY 2

THUGS CRY 3

TRUST NO BITCH

TRUST NO BITCH 2

TRUST NO BITCH 3

TIL MY CASKET DROPS

RESTRAINING ORDER

RESTRAINING ORDER 2

IN LOVE WITH A CONVICT

**Coming Soon**

BONDED BY BLOOD 2

BOW DOWN TO MY GANGSTA